BACK TO PLANET HOOLA

notionpress.com

BACK TO PLANET HOOLA

Sudipta Das

notionpress.com

Notion Press

5 Muthu Kalathy Street, Triplicane,

Chennai - 600 005

First Published by Notion Press 2013

ISBN: 978-93-83416-16-5

CONTENTS

1 RECAP

Hello, this is Dr. Adam Smith, psychiatrist and psychologist. Most of my career, I have been engaged as head of one of the world's leading mental health research centres and asylums. Perhaps, you have heard about my friend, Kit, the *asylum dweller*. I am talking about the one, who appeared virtually out of nowhere and, after spending two long decades in our asylum, disappeared mysteriously. He claimed to be an alien from another planet called Hoola, which is millions of light years away from the Earth. He left his diary to me. In the diary he gave vivid details and descriptions of his past life on that planet. Perhaps, you have read that diary too.

In case you have not read *The Asylum Dweller's Diary*, here is a quick recap. As written in the diary, this planet Hoola, along with eleven other planets, revolves around the nearest star called *Let*. Hoola has two natural satellites, named *Tin* and *Tar*. All the night skies of Hoola are lit up by either Tin or Tar. Everything about this planet, its calendar, landscape and innumerable diversity of flora and fauna, is quite strange and unlike those we find on Earth.

One of the unique and striking features of Hoola is this. Due to several physical reasons, including its planetary constellation, the egg-shaped atmosphere of the round shaped Hoola splits up the white light from *Let* into different colour rays. As a result, a given place on Hoola receives predominantly a particular colour of light during day time. The effect is somewhat like wearing coloured glasses. These strange colours change as one moves from one place on Hoola to another; like the red colour country Isthad, the blue colour country Inthad, the yellow colour country Hunthad and so on.

In his diary, Kit claims that he belongs to a mighty race, the *Hoos*, who inhabit Hoola. Strangely enough, the Hoos develop tails. However, their tails are quite unlike the tails that we see on Earth. A Hoo tail is much more evolved, superior, agile, sophisticated, sacred and coloured according to the ethnicity of the individual Hoo. The average height of the Hoos is about six feet but their tails grow up to eight feet long. So, for the convenience of their movement, the Hoos usually coil their tails around their bodies. In that position, their tails become indistinguishable with their bodies. Kit had purportedly lost his red colour tail in an incident before he had come to Earth.

Now, ten months have passed since Kit mysteriously disappeared from our asylum. The experiences, which I went through during the last seven months, are as fantastic, as mind-boggling and as fascinating as his diary. Also, there were interesting facts and events that took place meanwhile, in my absence, and I came to know about those subsequently. I have arranged all these chronologically to give you the continuous and complete story. It all started with an accident.

2

THE ACCIDENT

In all those twenty years while Kit was in our asylum I had employed all my professional knowledge and expertise and tried my best to cure his apparent psychological ailments. But, despite being an accomplished specialised doctor of international renown, I had failed to do so. I had been engrossed in trying to figure out the physiological and psychological causes of his bizarre behaviours and had found none. I realised later that the root of his eccentricity laid in an acute infection. It seemed that along with his diary, he had also passed on that infection to me. His infection was pure and unselfish affection.

I did not realise when I had become so fond of his friendship. In spite of my long experiences as a psychologist, I remained unaware of the delightful effects of his delightful personality on my own psyche. Is it because he is such a talented person? Or is it because that, he could easily and spontaneously connect to me at the higher planes of my psychic space where no one else could accompany my innermost loneliness?

After his disappearance, whenever I was not at work, I tended to miss his presence in our asylum and his memories occupied my consciousness. Days, weeks and months passed like this. Then, one day it all changed suddenly.

That day, I decided to give myself a break. I stacked my car with some sandwiches, canned food and drinks. Then I drove off to the north-eastern mountains, which are about twenty five kilometres away from our asylum. Soon, I was beyond the city limits and steered through the open countryside. I took the road that leads straight to the mountains. It was an early autumn morning. The sky was clear and at its most blue. On both sides of the road, there were paddy fields that stretched up to the green contours at the horizon. Farmers were busy at the fields, tending to their plants. Some of them knew me. They merrily waved at me and called out, "Hey Doc."

I waved back with a smile. The dispersed trees had just started to shed a few leaves. The fallen leaves were flown into the air as I sped past one of those trees. After a few kilometres more, the terrain became undulated and the road became wavy. Then, I reached the foot of the mountains. From there the serpentine road before me was narrower and uphill. As I drove higher through the lonely mountains, the air became chilly and a bit foggy. To my left the mountain slope rose up to the peaks and to my right was the sharp deep ravine. Gradually, the weather worsened further and visibility became low. I had visited the mountains several times before that day. I knew that in these mountains sometimes the weather changes quickly. So, with the hope that the weather would improve, I confidently negotiated the rather awkward road conditions. Ahead of me was a tricky U-turn. There was a wide trunked ancient oak at the rim of the turn. As I approached the turn, suddenly through the mist, appeared two human figures, a man and a lady.

They were few yards in front of my car, walking hand in hand and straight towards me. I reflexively pressed the car horn. But they were so engrossed with each other that they hardly seemed to notice my approaching car. Now, they were dangerously close. I kept pressing the horn and abruptly pulled the break. The mist had made the road slippery. My car skidded forward anyway.

At the last split second, the pedestrians moved aside, out of the way of my skidding car. As my car went past them, I could clearly see their fair and oval faces looking at me. I saw this exquisitely beautiful, bright blue-eyed, slim lipped stranger lady apparently in her mid-thirties. Her cheekbones were shapely rounded. Her hair was pony-tailed at the back of her head. Overall, she looked out of this world. The other face bore a sharp nose and these unmistakable calm brown eyes, serenely staring straight at my eyes, and wore a trademark childlike infectious smile at the corners of his pink lips. His long brownish hair cascaded from his crown down to his broad shoulders. Amazingly, he looked rejuvenated and as youthful as when I had met him for the first time at our asylum, twenty years earlier. He was about thirty-six then. Involuntarily, my gaze was fixed on his face. Looking backwards, I called out, "Ki … t".

Then I turned around and looked forward and saw that my car was still skidding ahead. It was perilously close to falling into the deep ravine beyond the outer edge of the sharp U-turn of the road. There was no time for me to open the car door and jump off the car. I grappled with my steering-wheel and barely managed to direct the car towards the old oak. My slipping car hit the oaken trunk at an angle, the front windshield shattered and my forehead hit hard on the steering wheel. Then the rear of the car turned half a circle and the car came to a halt with the rear wheels hanging in the air over the deep ravine.

I was dizzy. Everything around me appeared misty and hazy.

I hopelessly tried to figure out how to get out of the tottering car. Just then, a stretched masculine right hand appeared before me. Behind the hand were the two faces that I had seen a few seconds earlier. They were still pleasantly looking at me, apparently oblivious of my dire situation. Kit calmly said, "Here Doctor, hold my hand."

I stretched out my right hand and clasped his palm and he clasped mine. Then he pulled me up through the broken front windshield of the dangling car. Kit kept pulling me up as the car finally plunged into the ravine and disappeared in the mist below me. After several seconds, I heard the splashing sound of the car falling in the river below. In the meantime, all three of us, me, Kit and the blue eyed lady, kept moving through the mist. In that mist, I could not see anything other than my companions. I experienced enhanced G-force. Then, to my utter astonishment, I realised that we were moving but not walking on the road. We were moving in a direction, which, I felt, was upwards!

We turned, coasted, rolled and revolved through the seemingly endless mist. Kit held on to my clasp and, with all my strength, I held on to his palm. After several minutes, everything became dark. Now, I could not see anything. I only felt the warmth of Kit's palm in my grip. A strange stupefying feeling gripped me. I cannot exactly recall how long I was in that state. Probably, after a long while, a glimmer of light and the mist reappeared. However, this time, I felt like falling weightlessly through the mist. I glimpsed the burst of a strange joy on the faces of my companions. The air increasingly smelt unfamiliar. I wanted to ask Kit about what had been happening since he had rescued me from my dangling car. Before I could utter a word, I heard Kit calling out, "Hold on to me, Doctor. Take a deep breath. Hold your breath."

Within seconds, we were off the misty clouds. Still falling freely through the air, all I could see below us was endless tranquil blue waters. Then we awkwardly plunged into that water. The water felt cool, though not chilly, and sweet. So I presumed that we had fallen in some huge lake. As I struggled to reach the surface of the suffocating waters, Kit continued to extend his helping hand and pull me upwards. Just when the breathlessness had become too much to bear, I popped my head out of the surface of the waters. Instinctively, I puked a little of the water that I had swallowed and sucked up a breast full of air through my mouth.

Looking around, I saw water all around me, though I could not see very far as the sky was overcast with the clouds through which we had dropped. The only other objects that I saw were the heads of my two companions sticking out of the water. We constantly swam to keep ourselves afloat. Now, I said to Kit, "I did not know that this huge lake exists on the other side of the mountains. I have been to these mountains many times before. This place is only twenty five kilometres away from our asylum. Amazing, no one ever told me about it."

Kit smiled at me and said, "This is not on the other side of the mountains and this is not a lake. We are literally in the sea."

"Hey Kit, this is not the time for a joke. I have been to each and every continent. To the best of my knowledge there is no sweet water sea in the world," I said sternly.

"Maybe not in your world but here the seas naturally have sweet water. You are millions of light years away from your world. Welcome to my world, Doctor. Welcome to planet Hoola," said Kit.

3

BACK TO HOOLA

Astonished beyond my wits, I remained agape. Kit continued, "As soon as I breathed this air, the very breath of the air told me that I am back to Hoola. But I do not know in which sea and where on Hoola we are now."

"This way, please come along gentlemen." I heard the sweet voice of the beautiful lady for the first time. Kit nodded at me and I followed without asking a question. Kit put all his faith in the guidance of this stranger lady and I had no choice but to follow them. Our immediate necessity was to find dry land. She swam and Kit and I followed behind her. I had seen each and every style of swimming but I had never seen anyone swim the way she was swimming. As she moved at a steady pace, only her head was above the water but she left no ripples or waves behind her.

We did not talk much. The exhausting swim kept my mind occupied. After an hour or so, Kit excitedly said, "Doctor, look, dry land ahead."

I raised my head a bit above the waters and saw this beautiful violet aura at the horizon before me. I had never seen such natural violet colouration before that point in time. Kit continued, "Now I can guess that we are in the sea to the north of the Violet Land. I have lived in some of the southern parts of this land for about seven years. I know that bewildering, deserted and mostly arid land very well. But, I have never been to these northern regions of the land. I do not know what is waiting for us there."

Now the lady interrupted saying, "You will find out as you move on. Hurry up now. These waters are known to be the home of monstrous sea animals."

"That's true. Let's reach the shore as quickly as we can," said Kit.

The uneven sharp hilly features of the land became increasingly vivid as we approached nearer. After another half an hour or so, we reached near the shore. Here the tranquility of the sea was perturbed by the dangerous waves thrashing on the continental shelf. A huge wave washed all three of us ashore. Exhausted, I pulled myself up on a rock at the shore. My body felt much heavier than usual. Suddenly I recalled that Kit had written in his diary that Hoola is about four-thirds the size of Earth. Then I realised that the greater gravitational pull of Hoola made my body feel heavier than on Earth. Now, I was convinced that indeed I was on Hoola. I laid there with my back on the rock.

After catching some breath, I stood up and looked around. Behind me, I heard the rolling restless sea plunging its waves on the shore. Before me the rocky shoreline was embellished with sparse vegetation of strange exotic plants. The most striking of these were the palm like monocots vying for the sky, reaching up to fifty feet high. Beyond the trees, the landscape gradually rose with the peaks of the barren hilly terrain meeting the sky at the horizon. A few strange long beaked birds glided from one canopy to another. Their sharp shrill calls punctuated the roar of the sea. The scenario looked like an alien picture postcard dipped in violet colour. I remembered that I had read in Kit's diary that the daylight is predominantly violet in this Violet Land.

Now, I noticed my companions standing face to face on a rock at a distance. They seemed to be having a serious discussion. While approaching them I heard Kit anxiously say, "My love, you cannot just leave me like that. I cannot move an inch without you. Your affection is all the sustenance I need. What about the great deeds that we hope to accomplish together for the benefit of the race? "

"O my dearest Kit, I would never leave you if I could. This is how it is and it is beyond my control. I shall wait for you on the *other side*. Either you come and meet me there or you will have to call me back to this life by the power of your love. Hurry, if you are too late and I have to take another body and move on to the next life, then it will take centuries before we meet again." She paused briefly and continued, "You must find the hamlet at the green patch in the south of this Violet Land. We had desired to unite there before I was struck by my compatriot's arrow and was compelled to leave my body. From there, you must start anew." Then she softly said, "Don't be sad, my dear. All the light is in your own heart. May Almighty Intha bless you to realise that light and unleash its powers. May you grow in and with His divine solace."

I could not believe what I saw next. The blue eyed lady just faded away in the very air before Kit's anxious and teary eyes. I remained perplexed for a few moments.

Then I recalled. Kit had written to me in his parting letter, while he had mysteriously escaped from our asylum on Earth, that his beloved Ket's spirit often visited him in his cell number 121. That she would free him from the asylum. He had also written in that letter that, he and his beloved would remain on Earth until the right time comes. At the right time they would go back together to their planet, Hoola. It occurred to me now that this must be the right time. I realised that there must be some greater hidden cause behind everything that was happening.

I collected my thoughts and focused on the present. I went to the rock on which Kit stood all alone, silently staring at the air before him. I gently put my right palm on his left shoulder. He quietly turned his anguished face towards me. "My friend, remember the words she has just said. We have a lot of works to do," I said politely. Then, to pep up his mood, I animatedly added, "But first we must eat something. I feel very hungry, thirsty too. You must be hungry as well. I do not know this place. Can we find here something to eat?"

Coming to terms with his emotions, Kit calmly replied, "I hope so." Then pointing his right index, he added, "You see those violet shrubs over there. Those bear delicious fruits though the fruits may seem a bit strange to you."

Thus, we went on to survey the shores. We plucked and collected some fruits. And wow! Those were much more than just 'a bit strange' to me. One particular fruit looked truly alien. Its hard outer woody shell was actually the seed. The pulpy fruit was inside the seed. We had to break open the seed to get the pulp. "We call these *rok* fruits. Perhaps this is an evolutionary adaptation to cope with the harsh conditions of this rugged land," said Kit. Then he broke open the soft stem of a long grassy plant and handing over the same to me said, "Here, drink this, pure drinking water."

I sucked up the fluid from the tubular stem and quenched my thirst. We continued our conversation as we ate the strange but palatable fruits. "Hey Kit, can you please tell me what's going on? Am I dreaming or what?" I asked.

"Don't worry, Doctor. Everything is just the way you perceive it. It's all true. It's all okay," Kit calmly assured.

Then he pensively said, "According to the Hoo philosophy, we, the Hoos, are like the individual waves of the same infinite universal ocean; each of us trying to manifest a certain force into the external nature. Each of these forces is caused by earlier forces from within the ocean itself. It remains as a distinctive part of the ocean throughout its manifestation and then, after spending a lifetime, un-manifests and disappears in the body of the ocean. The wave disappears but its overtures, essence and spirit continues to remain in a subtle and finer state. For some time, it remains in this subtlety as a potent seed. Then, at the right time and under the right conditions, the seed sprouts and manifests its potency by taking another suitable body and a new wave is thus raised out of the universal ocean. Thus, the eternal and immortal individual Hoo spirit continues the cycle of life and death.

"Now, Ket's spirit had left her body after she was struck by an Inthadian arrow. But her unfulfilled love for me prevented her from moving on to take another form into the next life."

I interrupted saying, "Let me guess. She followed the call of your unfathomable love wherever you went. Her spirit remained with you even after you miraculously transcended millions of light-years from Hoola and landed on Earth. By dint of your utter sensitiveness and receptivity, only you could perceive Ket's spirit. Sometimes you even talked to her in your alien native language. Those, who saw you talking like that but could not see whom you were talking to, thought that you had some psychiatric disorder. That is why you were confined to cell number 121 of our asylum under my direct supervision. Twenty years went like this. During this time, I became a friend of yours. Then you mysteriously disappeared from our asylum."

Kit nodded and said, "That's exactly how it is. Only now you have grown sensitive enough to be able to see her spiritual being."

"I am awe stricken at the intensity of your mutual love with Ket," I said soberly. Then, I asked Kit, "But, till today, I have failed to understand how you managed to escape breaking the high gauge steel grid of the window of your cell and then defy the advanced surveillance system of our asylum. You must have used the rainwater pipe that runs along the window to climb down from your second floor cell. Didn't you? How could you remain under cover for months?"

Kit shook his head negatively and smilingly said, "No, no, it was not like the way you think. That night Ket came to me to keep her promise to take me out of your home. She just nudged the grid gently with the power of her super-material will. The high gauge steel grid of the window snapped like fine fabric. Then she took my hands in her hands, scooped me out of the window and flew me to the secluded mountains in the dark of the night. We remained there in each other's loving company."

"That's incredible!" I exclaimed in utter disbelief.

Kit smiled and then said in a serious mood, "Doctor, the work at hand is going to be physically demanding. The hamlet is at a green patch of land in the southern part of this Violet Land. Finding the green patch in this rugged dry land will not be easy. It will be hard for you to take the toil at this age. You can wait for me here. You have enough food, water and shelter here. I shall get back to you after I find the way to the hamlet."

"No way, don't worry about me," I opposed. "I can pull it off. I know our progress will be a bit slower if I come along, but we will have the advantage of two minds working together. You said that you know those southern regions."

"Yeah, but to reach there, first we have to cross the northern regions. These areas are mostly unknown. Many lost their way and their lives in this bewildering maze," said Kit.

"Surely we can do better with a little plan and preparation," I opined.

"Sure. We shall have to gather at least two weeks supply of food, water and provisions before we can start," suggested Kit.

For the next few days we devoted all our energies in the preparations for the journey. We collected the exotic fruits; caught and smoked the flesh of strange mouse-like small animals, which Kit called *rodns*. The hard shells of the *rok* fruits proved to be good containers for carrying water. We even constructed a small trolley with the bushy branches of the *bem* trees for carrying our provisions. Kit suggested that we should move during the night and rest at daytime. He explained that at night, the white light from either of the two natural satellites of Hoola, Tin and Tar, makes the conditions of the Violet Land more suitable for navigation.

Thus we set out one evening towards the south to traverse the uncertainty that lay beyond the horizon where the peaks of the barren mountains meet the sky. It was reassuring for me to see that indeed Kit was pretty good at finding the ways through these undulated alien landscapes. With apparent ease he carefully observed the rocky formations of the terrain ahead of us and deftly chose the easiest way forward. Even that easiest way was pretty strenuous for me. From time to time, Kit had to stop and wait for me to catch up with him. Fortunately, Kit's efforts bore positive results. We stumbled upon a pass through the skyscraping mountains. By daybreak I was pretty tired. We made our first halt in a cave near the pass.

After resting for the day we recommenced our journey at about dusk. At the end of the pass beyond the mountains we were faced with a rapid descent. Kit would not allow me the risks of trying to go down that steep descent. I was not very confident either. It seemed too formidable. So we changed our direction and moved along the mountain slope towards the east. We had to cover several kilometres before we could find what we were looking for, a gradual descent down to the plateau. After coming down to the plateau, we again changed our direction towards the south. If I was not with him, probably, Kit would have gone straight towards the south down that steep descent. But, this change of the trek would soon lead us to an interesting discovery.

After covering several kilometres towards the south, we saw something ahead of us that looked like a huge carcass of an ancient beast lying amidst the desert in the soothing light of *Tar*. As we went nearer, we found it to be the remains of a very old abandoned factory. We picked up a few useful articles including a piece of blunt metal blade from the factory. Kit carefully grinded the metal on a rough rock and attached a handle to it. With this handcrafted sword fastened to his waist he indeed looked like a warrior, just like he had described in his diary.

Kit remarkably said to me, "This is clear evidence that once, a long time ago; there was a sprawling habitation on the Violet Land. This belies the general belief prevailing on both sides of the Violet Land that there has never been any habitation on this land. It also shows that conditions on at least some parts of the Violet Land must have been hospitable in the past and that there is water somewhere near this place."

"Congratulations!" I said.

"Same to you, we found it together. One day, all of Hoola will know about this," said Kit. "Now, let us look for that water source. If we find it then we can replenish our supplies."

Thus we went about looking for this source of water. But, after hours of searching, all that we could find on that flat and arid terrain were mostly sand and stones. Dawn approached and we decided to rest for the day. As we ate our breakfast before going to sleep, scattered crystalline stones shone in the violet light of the rising *Let*. At first Kit did not take much notice. Then suddenly something struck in his mind and apparently he became curious. He stood up, walked a few steps and picked up one of those stones. Holding the stone before his eyes he closely examined it. Then, he hurriedly came back to me. Handing over the stone to me, he exclaimed, "See what I have found!"

I turned the stone in my fingers and asked, "What's this?"

Kit animatedly replied, "Those sands must be the dried up remains of a river bed. These spear shaped crystal stones tell me exactly which river, the Forbidden River."

"What!" I exclaimed. I had read about this river in Kit's diary.

"Yes Doctor, these are the same kind of crystal stones that I saw in the dried up Forbidden River at the foot of the Forbidden Mountain," said Kit.

"That means if we follow the trail of these stones then we will reach the foot of the Forbidden Mountain," I said.

"Yes. I know that place. The hamlet is only a few kilometres south-west from there!" exclaimed Kit.

Within a few days after that we reached the hamlet.

4

RESURRECTION

The initial days and weeks at the hamlet were difficult. We felt severe resources crunch. We virtually had to scavenge on whatever we could find at the, now deserted, hamlet. We found a few utensils, some soiled agricultural tools and a worn-out chest containing a few household articles and clothes. Luckily for us, in the field, there were uncultivated crops, which had naturally grown and regrown over the passing seasons. Harvesting those scattered crops was a herculean task. There was water in the tanks but we mostly relied on fresh rainwater for drinking. We mended and hatched two of the huts that were in relatively better condition.

Within a few weeks, we were able to secure a buffer stock of food and provisions though we still led a hard life at the margin of subsistence. All along, Kit exhibited his characteristic activeness and maintained his overt cheerfulness. But, I did not require my long experiences as a psychologist to be able to detect the undercurrent of melancholy that had been tormenting him from inside ever since Ket had disappeared.

Increasingly, now Kit spent as much of the spare time as possible in alignment and submission to his deity, Istha. Usually he aligned in the solitude of his hut but sometimes, even while at work, I found him absentmindedly looking skywards and murmuring prayers with such acute intensity, which I had not seen in anyone else before that point in time.

Then one day early in the morning, Kit rushed to my hut and knocked at the door. I got up from my bed, opened the door and I asked him, "What's the matter?"

With a childlike excitement and exuberance Kit said in one breath, "Doctor, I had a contact with gracious Istha this dawn. He blessed me. He has given me a hope of getting Ket back."

I could hardly believe what he had said but I knew that each of his words came from the depths of truth. So, I said, "Come inside. Tell me in detail."

Once inside my hut, we sat down. Kit continued, "After the midnight before this morning, I engaged in a session of alignment and submitted my being to Istha. I remained calm and quiet for a long while. Then, the spirituality of the Deity arouse in my consciousness. My crown was filled with the Divine's beautiful effulgent light. Overwhelmed by rapturous joy, I humbly conveyed to Istha, 'Just when darkness seems to engulf my being and I, degraded by my ignorance, tend not to remember Thy glory and thus give way to despair, that Thee, my kindest Lord, manifest Thyself in all Thy greatness and grandeur and dispel with Thy divine light the minutest of doubt from my consciousness.'

"Then I heard the soothing Divine voice say, 'My dear Kit, despair not. I am ever with you and I am ever with all; my love is unceasing. I bless you with the bliss of my love.'

"I humbly maintained my submission, silence and focus. The Divine continued, 'Now listen carefully. I will convey the *death defying verses of resurrection* directly into your memory. But you shall not transfer it to anyone else. You can recite and use it only once. After that it will be permanently lost from your memory. You must remain pure. Recover Ket's body and recite the verses at the next twilight when neither of Tin and Tar will be in the sky. The verses will make the way for Ket's spirit to re-enter her body.'

"Within the next split second, I received the stanzas long *death defying verses of resurrection*. I was about to express my gratefulness but Istha's spiritual effulgence dispersed into the subtler realms of my consciousness and transcended beyond my perception. But I still vividly remember the long verses."

I immediately recalled that Kit had written in his diary that he had buried Ket's body at the peak of the Forbidden Mountain just before he had gone to Earth. *What will be the state of the body now?* I wondered. But I suppressed my apprehension and said, "The Mountain is several kilometres away from this hamlet and then there is that arduous climb to the top. Let us start immediately."

I wanted to witness the miracle but Kit forbade me saying, "You stay here and wait for me. I shall be faster if I go alone."

I saw the reason. I could not run or climb as quickly as Kit. So I said, "Then waste no time, my friend. I shall wait here and pray for both of you. Bring her back to life and bring her back to her future home. Best of luck, Kit."

Before I could finish my words, Kit was up from his seat and running. I went up to my doorstep to see him off.

Standing at the threshold of my hut, I lost sight of him behind a couple of old bushy *bem* trees. Soon *Let* was up in the sky showering its violet light upon the loneliness of the rustic landscapes of the green patch around me. It was difficult for me to focus on the chores. All sorts of thoughts came to my mind. Anxiety gripped me. I could not eat the whole day. Then *Let* went down at the horizon in the opposite direction to which Kit had gone.

Past twilight, I knew that whatever had to happen must have happened by now. When Ket's soul had left her body Kit had almost taken his own life. *What would he do if he failed to resurrect her now?* I wondered. *I should not have let him go alone.* I thought.

Hungry, I took a few sips of self-made grain soup and retired to bed. But sleep would delude me. I kept turning from one side to the other in my bed. I decided that I would go out to look for Kit if he did not return within two hours of the next daybreak. Accordingly, I got up from my bed before the daybreak. I cleaned up the areas around Kit's hut and decorated it with a few wild flowers that had blossomed during the night. I also kept a couple of flower garlands ready with the hope of their return.

Then, I walked towards the east to the twin *bem* trees and sat down below one of those. From there, I could see up to the elevation of the hills at the horizon in the violet aura of the dawn. Soon the upper rim of the violet disc of *Let* popped up on the horizon; then a quarter, then the upper half and then the full disc was at the horizon. My heartbeats were going up with the rising *Let*. The scenery was simply breathtaking but the anxiety of the passing moments almost took my breath away.

After that, it was sheer magic. On the violet disc of *Let* appeared the dark contours of the two beings that I was, so eagerly, looking for. Unable to hold on to my joy, I waved and ran towards them and they came running down towards me.

Even today, I sometimes tend to wonder how I could become so emotionally attached to two individuals who are supposed to be aliens to me. What is this agent that brought people from two different distant worlds, me and them, to such close proximity? So much so, that I felt quite at home in this rugged land on this bizarre planet millions of light years away from my home on Earth. That would be clear to me soon afterwards.

Now, Kit and his beloved were standing before me, hand in hand, with their jubilant smiles and joyful eyes lighting up their faces. Kit said, "Doctor, by the grace of Almighty Istha, we made it." Then he formally introduced me to his lady saying, "This is Ket, my life-bird."

I exchanged greetings with her and said, "Now we have two doctors at the hamlet, madam."

I knew that, like me, Ket was a doctor too. She nodded and smiled. I joyously told them, "I feel so relieved. I feel so happy for you. I cannot believe my eyes."

Then I asked Kit, "How did you make her alive again?"

Kit said to me, "Here is a little open secret. She has always been alive in my heart."

They smilingly looked at each other's eyes, stepped closer and put their hands around each other's waist. Then, turning to me, Kit continued, "I made it to the top of the Forbidden Mountain just before twilight.

Wasting no time, I dug up her body from the burial. The conditions at the Mountain peak had perfectly preserved her buried body and so frozen her age at her mid-thirties, as old as she had been when the arrow had stricken her. Then, twilight came. Neither of *Tin* and *Tar* was in the sky. As I chanted the *death defying verses of resurrection*, the wound at her back healed and her body was filled with fresh blood. Now, just as Istha had said, the passage was opened for her soul to re-enter and re-claim her body."

Awe-stricken, I exclaimed, "Wow, it's a miracle!"

I handed over the flower garlands that I had made for them. They merrily put the garlands around each other's neck. Then I serenely continued, "I do not know how a marriage is solemnised in your community, if at all. I am also aware that such a marriage between a blue Inthadian female and a red Isthadian male may be unprecedented. In any case, I do not possess any legal authority to declare you husband and wife. But, nevertheless, I wish and pray from the bottom of my heart that may you remain happily ever in union."

They thanked me. Ket welcomed me saying, "It's a privilege to have you as our honoured guest, Doctor."

Thereafter, I took their leave for the day, leaving them in their mutual loving company.

5
LOVE DIVINE

Thus Kit and Ket blissfully settled down in each other's companionship and happiness descended upon the humble hamlet. The fragrance of their love energised every element around them. Their incredibly subtle rapport was particularly evident when they sang. I often heard them spontaneously singing these amazingly melodious duets even as they did their respective chores. Even though I had just started to learn their Hoo language a bit, I could not comprehend the exact meaning of the lyrics. Nevertheless, I could make out from their expressions and their application of the notes that these were love songs. One particular of these duets sounded incredibly beautiful to me. So, Kit translated the original lyric for me, from the Hoo language to English. It goes as follows:

Because of Thee-
I be.

At every single moment,
Thou makest me.

Thou art Divine
And so is me
And so is all
That me-shares with Thee.

With Thy
Selfless love,
Transform me
Into a peaceful dove.

Let Thy spark
Fire my resolve–
To embrace all–
Below, at and above.

Play me
As Thou playest Thy flute–
And let Thy work
Be done through me.

Blissful presence eternal
And for ever free;
Thou art in me
And me is in Thee.

Because of Thee,
I be.

The original lyric in the Hoo language rhymes, rhythms and recites even better. *Is this expression of love? Or is this worship? Or is this both, each merged into the other?* I wondered.

One of these days, Kit told me, "You know, Doctor, all love, affection, pleasures and even transient, apparently silly, infatuations disseminate from the Divine. The differences are only in the level, degree and form. The Divine, out of His love, manifested as the material and the subtle forms of this universe. From that instant 'time' came into existence. Therefore, it is only natural that the various components of the universe would exhibit that affinity among themselves, everything and everyone being of the same Divine essence. Mother, father, sister, brother, daughter, son, friend, lover, the Divine appears in all the forms to give and receive His love. *The Lover is Divine, the Beloved is Divine and, in a subtle form, Their Love is also Divine."*

"Of these, one form of love has stood out as the most chronicled in the folklore, mythology, memoir, art, literature and legend of every culture; that between the lover and the beloved," I commented.

Kit nodded, smiled and said, "That is because the spontaneous love of the lover for the beloved has a striking feature. It is neither created nor caused by any deliberation by the lover or evoked by any particular quality in the beloved. Though rare, it just strikes you and when it strikes you, you know that it is there, as if, it has always been there hidden somewhere and under the right conditions, at the right time it manifests itself in its most delightful manner. Just as this love cannot be created, neither can it be destroyed. The Hoo history stands as evidence that, sword cannot cut this love, fire cannot burn it and water cannot dissolve it. As you know now, it remains undiminished from a thousand kilometres away, even from light years away, from another corner of the universe through eternity.

"I am lucky that I got struck by this pure love, a great gift directly from the Divine. When it happened to me, as I swayed and swung in its enormous descending and ascending waves of struggle, dismay and sheer ecstasy, I knew for sure that the Supreme Lord had just opened up an avenue to lead me directly unto Himself; an opportunity for instant divinisation, spiritual ascent and ecstasy. *My love leads me to the being of my beloved and, through the beloved, to the Divine Unity that lies behind."*

They had tremendous respect for each other's *colour*. Sometimes Kit made a blue choker with the dried skin of a kind of blue creeper and wore it around his neck. Ket would extract the pigments of a wild fragrant scarlet flower and put on a red colour spot between her eyebrows. The red spot contrasted beautifully with her deep blue eyes. Sometimes, she wore a stitch-less red bordered white cloth that was found in the old chest.

Usually, they bathed in the morning. Then they engaged in alignment to their respective Deities and recited these wonderful sounding verses in their Hoo language. Thereafter, they had their breakfast. Kit devoted the next few hours to his work in the field. In the evening, he worked for the harmony of the race. The work that Kit aspired to accomplish was formidable; to create a book that would dispel the apparent contradictions in the externalities of the different colours and reveal the subtle unity of their underlying principles. But, Ket remained by him like an unshakable and unflinching pillar of support, a fountain of pure inspiration. Sometimes she ran her delicate fingers through Kit's luxuriant hair, caressed his face and reassured him saying, "Lord Intha is always with us and He will surely allow you to do His work. I am so fortunate that I am witnessing His work being done through you, my love!"

Then Kit would say, "Like a piece of straw following every movement of the waves in a stream and like the pebbles that roll beneath it, I have been following the proprieties that this external world threw up at me at every moment. Giving little heed to the world that is within, I took this externality for granted and have ever been serving it thus. Little did I realise that the One, who is within, is the Soul Divine, the very projection of the Supreme Being. Hidden behind the veils of illusion, the call of the Divinity from within the heart has mostly remained unheard. At your very advent, my love, the illusory curtains were dispelled at once and the pristine light of truth came through. In your association, the inner call has become so loud that it can no longer be ignored. It has become so obvious and it is amazing how it remained hidden for so long.

"Now, I realise that you are no weakness of mine, but strength. There is no falling but only awakening and arising in this love. My dear Ket, you embolden me to take on the external anomalies from inside out."

Ket's catalytic effect on Kit's psyche expanded his consciousness manifolds and in all dimensions; in height, in width as well as in depth. Rapidly, he grew a new colour changing Hoo tail. His unique eight feet long tail turned to the colour of the *Colour Deity* to which he aligned and submitted himself. At times, his tail became invisible altogether when he aligned himself to his own internal Self. Kit would fervently maintain that every Hoo was potent to develop such a tail if it could understand the unique essence of each *colour* and realise the relativity that exists among the *colours*. According to him, a Hoo only needed to remain pure and unattached in its mind in order to be able to achieve these. What he did not say, however, was that a Hoo is required to be perseverant like him as these things do not happen overnight.

I became so motivated by Kit's awe inspiring achievements that, for months at a stretch, I committed myself to alignments and submissions to their *Colour Deities*. Kit readily helped me with these. These alignments brought me internal peace. But, in spite of my sincere efforts I did not develop a tail. After all, they are an alien race and I am a human being. Humans do not develop tails.

I had read in Kit's diary that, Kit and Ket had first met as children in their classroom. A few years after that, they had to part when they were boy and girl. They had remained separated for many years. The experiences that they had gone through during their years of separation were vastly diverse. Now, they had a chance to exchange those experiences and thus enrich themselves. These two love-birds often engaged in confabulations on various topics, from the most trivial to the most intense and illuminating. Of course, they also talked about their mutual personal affairs and freely expressed their feelings for each other.

Even after hours of such verbal engagement, they remained so fresh, jolly and animated that it seemed as if they had just started talking. However, these seemingly effortless discourses were much more than mere sweet pastime. Their mutual affection caused each to eagerly listen to and instantaneously internalise what the other had to say. Even the points of differences were sweetly harmonised by their spirit of mutual acceptance. At times their discussions brought forth such wonderful wisdoms as well as their own realisations.

Listening to them, I sometimes thought that, *they were tailor-made for each other by the Supreme and united by His master design.* Each was perfectly aware of the other's mind. At times they seemed like one mind in two bodies.

Neither of them imposed any condition on the other. This freedom was a key to their relationship. Kit had once sagely said, "In freedom, flourishes love."

Being a psychologist, sometimes I wondered, *if their love overtly appears so intense and beautiful, how do they conceive, perceive and feel this love in their own minds and in their hearts?*

I did not have to wait for long to get the answer. One day, during a leisurely stroll through the field, Kit dispelled my curiosity. What he said that day, in a nutshell, is as follows:

Their unconditional and unselfish love for each other exalted their consciousnesses and filled them with the love and the bliss of the Supreme Being. Their love bears the same qualities and is of the same spiritual matter as the love of the Supreme; *unilateral, unconditional* and *unselfish.*

The Supreme is not only the Parent as well as the Creator of this universe but It is the universe itself. Its love for Its children, for Its creation and for Itself, is *unilateral.* No matter what we, Its wards, commit or omit, Its *unconditional* love for us never ceases. The Supreme has nothing to gain from us but It never fails to shower Its *unselfish* love upon us.

Their consciousnesses were always filled with the delightful existence of each other's being. Even their physicality culminated into super sensuous bliss. When they united in love embracing each other, their tails tangled. Their deepest secrets were revealed to each other. There was no sense of having and taking in either one of them; only an acute desire for giving. Each was pleased at the other's pleasure. Then their consciousnesses played, mingled and merged into a tango of super sensuous bliss and their souls became one inseparable whole full of such ecstasy that easily subordinated all other pleasures.

Such is the prize of unconditional and unselfish love. Lover, Beloved and Love itself, all became One, each of the three being of the same kind and of the same spiritual matter. They were thus divinised.

The Supreme is love.

Love is the Supreme.

The Supreme loves love.

Kit also told me that their love was a precious gift directly from the Supreme and that it had a special purpose for its existence. With the fruits of this love they would have to serve the entire Hoo race.

Their love has fascinatingly combined the two and elevated their finite consciousnesses so high that they have become infinitely more powerful, I realised.

6

THE TWINS

The outcome of their divine love could only be divine. About a year after their marriage, they were blessed with two angelic twins, a female and a male. The arrival of the twins immediately added new dimensions to their bliss and brought in lifestyle changes. Now Ket devoted all her energies in attending to her babies. Kit helped her and did most of the outdoor chores.

Like all newly born Hoo babies, the twins were tailless. They grew up pretty fast. In a year and a half, they were walking, talking and, perhaps taking a cue from their parents, even singing. Ket taught them to address me as uncle. They became friendly with me. Sook, their son, and Soor, their daughter, were born with the perfection, which Kit and Ket had aspired for and had realised through their life long endeavours, alignments and prayers. In the Hoo language, *Sook* means tranquil, serene, equanimous, stoic, and those were exactly the qualities that Sook exhibited. The unshakable calmness of his mind enabled him to have tremendous power of concentration. Nothing in and around him could distract his composure unless he allowed his mind to veer from the point of his focus. He could effortlessly remain focused on an object for days at a stretch.

Soor, on the other hand, means sublime delight, affection and beauty in the Hoo language. Those were the perfected nature with which their daughter was born. She spoke sweeter than the sweetest bird that you may have ever heard. She was so endearing that the lotus-like transparent *crystal flowers* blossomed and turned their faces towards her whenever she passed by them. The six-winged *rainbow flies* merrily hovered around her. The little *pic* birds ceased their quarrelsome chirping and sang in unison with her whenever she sang. The very breeze became fragrant in her delightful presence.

It was amazing to see how the two alien beings happily raised their twin offspring; that life could be so simple and yet, bliss could be so blissful and ecstasy so ecstatic! The heavens descended on their hamlet and they lived in it like the heavenly beings, the gods and the goddesses.

One day, the eternal lad, Sook, said to his mother, "O Ma, you have taken so much pain in bearing me and my sister, Soor, and to bring us to this world."

Ket lovingly replied with a smile, "My dearest, it is true that I went through the pleasure, the toil, the exhaustion, the anticipation and the apprehension while bearing you and the extreme physical pain when you were born. But then, when I saw your faces for the first time, my entire being was filled with this utter, immense and super-sensuous bliss which easily surpassed all the previous experiences. I earnestly thanked Almighty Intha for blessing me with you." Then the mother kissed the lad on his forehead.

Sometimes I told the twins about Earth and humanity. They heard me with curiosity in their innocent eyes.

Their serious education though, naturally came from their outstanding parents.

One of these days in the morning, Ket called out at them, "Come to me dearest children, today I shall tell you how the blue Inthadians align themselves to their deity, Intha."

The tiny tots huddled towards their mother. Ket lit a blue torch and fixed it on the ground. Then, pointing her gorgeous long blue tail towards the torch she said, "Follow me as I demonstrate. First face the blue light of Intha. Now, with the tips of your right fingers touch your foreheads. Focus your concentration in your heads, the seat of your intellects. Pray that the infinite knowledge of Intha expands your intellects.

"Then lower your right hands and touch the centres of your chests, wherein is enshrined your hearts, the centres of your affections. Focus in the heart of your hearts. Pray that Intha may fill your hearts with His all-encompassing love.

"After that, move your right fingers to touch your left shoulders and draw the fingers horizontally to your right shoulders. These horizontal lines represent the *balance* between your heads and your hearts. Pray that Intha may bless you with this most important *balance* and thus, guide you through your lives from within yourselves."

Another day, the kids gathered around their father to learn the technique and secret of alignment that is more akin to the Isthadians. First, Kit gave them a brief discourse about a broader perspective of the *colours* saying, "The knowledge of the blissful truth of the Divine, who reside in every heart, mostly remain unknown to the Hoos. Most of them often quarrel about the external forms of the *colours* without understanding their underlying essences and principles.

"The mind space is like a lake. To be able to see what is at the bottom of this lake, the water must be calm and bereft of all motion. But the external stimuli enter the mind space through the senses and raise the waves of impressions, which make the water of the lake turbulent. Therefore, our task is to calm and quiet the mind. To do this, the great Hoo Originators have devised the different *colours* and advised different techniques of alignment. The aim of all these techniques is the same; to realise the Self Divine.

"The Isthadian technique is like this. First, take a comfortable posture and physically align yourself to the red *colour deity,* Istha. Then close your eyes and detach your mind from the senses by focusing on your breathings and thus, still your nerves. Next, stop all the mental activities and switch off the noise of thoughts in your mind."

The kids carefully listened and followed their father's instructions.

Kit continued, "Now, after you have detached yourselves from your physical and mental beings, remain as a mute neutral observer of what is going on in the mind. Do not try to do anything deliberately. If you continue to follow this method regularly and persevere for long enough, one day, you will surely discover the ever effulgent Divinity in the heart of the heart of your own Selves."

After the alignment session, Kit sagaciously advised his children, "My dear kids, remember that the Hoo Originators revealed the different *colours* and methods that worked the best for their respective Selves in their respective times and places. All the external forms, suggestions and *colours* are there only to help you as props. Ultimately, it is entirely up to you to decide which *colour* or *combination of colours* you want to pursue to uniquely realise the divinity of your own Self."

Kit once told Ket, "What is the use of giving only lip service to the cause of the universal whole while overly contaminating our offspring with the limited and partial impressions of existence, which we have unavoidably inherited as a legacy of the past?

"It is perhaps more a matter of inevitability, than anything else, that while a newborn Hoo grows up, it naturally imbibes the *colour* in which it is born and brought up. By the time the child reaches adulthood, a major portion of its consciousness is already filled with the essence and the culture of the *colour*. Moreover, through the habits grown over years of conditioning, particularly during the early, tender and impressionable years, the *colour*, consciously, subconsciously or unconsciously, affects not only the Hoo's thoughts, words and actions, but also every other aspect of its being. Thus preoccupied with its own *colour*, the individual Hoo being becomes un-accommodative to the other *colours* in its mental space. So, often one becomes biased and prejudiced, without even being aware of it, as the *colour* percolates and sits deep within one's psychology and controls one from there.

"While certain effects of this *colour conditioning* are immensely beneficial, others are equally devastating. It's most ill effect is the fragmentation of the Hoo race into these numerous *colours* and their innumerable *sub-colours*, *hues* and *shades*. The apparent and external differences of the *colours* have further aggravated this fragmentation, which has taken the ugly shape of the inter *colour conflicts*."

7

THE WORK

As I have already written, when we had first reached the green patch in the Violet Land, we were compelled to survive with whatever we could scavenge in and around the hamlet. We knew that this scavenging would not sustain us in the long run. So, soon after arriving at the hamlet, Kit and I started cultivating a piece of the fertile land.

The Hoos are a technologically far advanced race than the humans. But, the tools that Kit and I were using now looked primitive even by human standards. We had to manage with whatever small implements were available. The works were tedious and laborious.

Everything on that land was so strange. Even the air smelt strange, though soothing. Kit had told me that it was the smell of the leaves of the plants that we cultivated. In the beginning, I had to focus a lot even to do the most ordinary of tasks. Things, which I had automatically performed on Earth, had to be thought out before those could be executed on Hoola. I often consulted Kit and later on, Ket regarding the daily chores. Moreover, I was about fifty-six and became easily exhausted. They, on the other hand, were in their self-terrain, like fish in water. Also, Kit had been rejuvenated back to his mid-thirties. His reunion with Ket had filled him with such invigorating joy that made him ten times stronger than an average Hoo. He readily and happily bore much of the burden of the labour. He is such a jolly good fellow. Sometimes, he cheerfully hummed these wonderful Hoo romantic songs to himself while working.

All along, in spite of doing the lion's share of the chores that were at hand, Kit, somehow, managed some time every day for alignment and continued his work with the *vision of harmony* of the race. His aphorism was '*One Hoola and one Hoo race*'.

I had read in Kit's diary, written while he was in our asylum, that, Kit had already realised several *Colour Deities* including the Violet Deity, the violet manifestation of the one and only Supreme Being, while he was in captivity in Inthad. There were about three hundred *colour countries* of all shades and hues on *Hoola* but none of them was *violet.* Violet was traditionally thought to be the forbidden colour. Now Kit had busted that myth. He revealed the wonderful and auspicious aspects of the Violet Deity.

But, with great resolve and wisdom, he consciously controlled the temptation to become an Originator and refrained from formulating the Violet *colour*, which would add another *colour* to the already existing plethora of *colours* mutually competing for exclusive supremacy. He realised that the Hoo race was already divided enough by the *colours*. The *colours* were to serve, in their respective ways, their purpose of aligning the Hoo spirit towards the truth of the Supreme. However, due to their diverse approaches to the Absolute Truth, the *colours* often evoked *colour conflicts,* the single greatest cause of feuds, genocides, battles and wars. *Augmenting one more 'name', 'form' and 'colour' would only aggravate the division of the Hoo race.*

Kit realised that something else was the call of the hour; something that would bring home and demonstrate the inherent *harmony* among the apparently different *colours.*

Kit's enormous heart melted with such piety and compassion for the entire Hoo race. The fluid pumped up and came out through his eyes in the form of a colourless, saline and degenerative liquid. With this liquid, he aspired to draw a vibrant and colourful picture potent with the forces of harmony and leave an indelible mark in the collective Hoo psyche of the race.

One day, I overheard Kit earnestly pray, "O Lord, the task before me is so enormous that I find myself humbled. Every aspect of my being seems so average that, looking at myself, I sometimes wonder, how average, average can be? But, everything that You have given me, I put forth at Your service. Use me, use me the way You like and please do not consider what may happen to me. O my kindest Lord, just let me do your work."

Looking skywards, he often absent-mindedly murmured the following words to himself.

"O the Supreme,
Set me in Thy eternal note and

Let me awaken all in this world,
Pouring in Thy immortal love."

Praying thus, Kit proceeded to propound his realisation of the great theory of harmony that lies behind the *colours*. In the Hoo language, Kit means *servant to the Supreme*. True to his name, Kit plunged himself in the inspired service to the Supreme Being with such selfless dedication and zeal.

8

THE ANCIENT STONE-TABLETS

Meanwhile, Sook and Soor have been growing up merrily. Although they seldom complained about anything, the scopes for their entertainment at the hamlet were rather limited. Hoo children, elsewhere on technologically advanced Hoola, had a fantastic array of games and shows for their amusements. Kit sometimes took the family on outings into the mazy rugged wilderness of the Violet Land beyond the periphery of the green patch. He wanted to playfully acquaint the kids with the realities of the Violet Land while they had a nice time. At times, I also joined these picnic parties.

The other day, we planned to visit the Forbidden River at the foot of the Forbidden Mountain. The kids were thrilled. Tit-bits and refreshments were packed. After having our breakfast that morning, we set off towards the horizon, above which, hovered *Let*. We reached there well before *Let* reached the zenith. Kit carefully selected a vantage-point for our camp. The view of the landscape was simply spectacular, just as Kit had described in his diary. Before us was the sandy bed of the, now dried up, Forbidden River embellished with spear-shaped, crystalline stones pointed upwards. In the violet light of *Let*, those crystalline stones sparkled creating an illusion of waves and ripples. Beyond the river bed, the magnificent Forbidden Mountain rose up to the sky almost like a straight wall. Ket said to the kids, "Beyond this mountain is Inthad, the blue *colour country* where I was born."

Kit pointed to the peak of the mountain and said, "There, Ket and I reunited." Then he turned to Ket and exchanged affectionate smiles.

The kids were very happy. We watched them from the camp at what might have been the bank of the river a long time ago. They delightfully roamed about on the river bed at a distance and played with the diamond-like crystals. Soor hummed this beautiful tune breaking into the utter silence of the place and adding to the experience of the breathtaking beauty of the surroundings.

After about an hour or so, the kids came back to us running, first Sook, followed by Soor. They were holding some objects in their hands. Sook handed over a tile-like object to Kit and said, "Look Pa, what I have found!"

Ket and I watched as Kit carefully turned and examined the opaque, almost square shaped stone-tablet broken slantingly at one side. Then Soor gave him a similar piece and animatedly said, "I have found this."

Kit intuitively held the broken slanting sides of the two pieces together. Those matched perfectly forming a rectangular shape of about two feet by one foot. Kit held the one inch thick stone tablet before us and said, "This is striking. These stones do not belong to this place. All the natural stones found here are transparent crystals. Somebody must have brought these here."

Then he gently placed the tablet on the ground and wiped off the dust from its surface with his furry tail.

Now there were even more surprises. We found almost faded away unknown scripts inscribed on the tablet. Kit excitedly said, "These are the ancient scriptures of this region. These stone-tablets must be at least three thousand years old. At around that time, this ancient language had become extinct. It has certain similarities to our present Hoo language of the region. I shall try to read these. If I am guessing right, then there must be more such stones here. These stones have an unknown story to tell. It will be great if I can find the full story."

Indeed, Kit's guess was right. After searching the place for another couple of hours we found two more such stone-tablets. Thus, thanks to Sook and Soor, our fun-filled outing, accidentally, ended up in an interesting 'find'. We left our camp intact to mark the site of the find and came back to our hamlet with the stone-tablets.

Thereafter, Kit devoted most of his spare time to the tablets. He visited the site several times. He excavated many places at and around the site and recovered many more such inscribed ancient stone-tablets. We were intrigued to know why he was so much engrossed in the stones. But, knowing him, we knew that he knew what he was doing. After months of painstakingly working with the tablets, Kit was able to decipher the ancient scriptures and make out the full story that the stones had to tell. In fact, it turned out to be a crucial piece of lost Hoo history of this region on Hoola; a fascinating history that would subsequently prove to be immensely significant to the estranged relations between Inthad and Isthad.

Kit told us, "I do not know who recorded these truths on the stones. But someone who wanted to suppress these truths must have thrown the stone tablets into the Forbidden River when it was full of water. We may never know who it was or what its motives were but its ploy has surely been foiled now. Truth has this uncanny habit of opening, sooner or later. All of Hoola, particularly, Inthad and Isthad, must know these truths. We have to prepare to go to Isthad."

"Wouldn't it be risky? You are not very popular there," observed Ket.

"We have to take the risk for a higher cause. We will go to Nik's hamlet in Isthad," affirmed Kit. Such is his nature; always ready to sacrifice for the sake of others.

9

GOING TO NIK, THE WISE, IN ISTHAD

The Violet Land is situated between Isthad and Inthad. The green pasture, on which our hamlet is located, is towards the eastern side of the Violet Land bordering Inthad. Isthad is beyond the western side of the Land. It would take about fifteen days to reach there. I had read in Kit's diary that, years ago, he had developed the inner sight necessary to navigate the bewildering maze of the Violet Land beyond our pasture. He had led a caravan in this path to Isthad and had left a trail of marks along the way. Now we were to retrace that trail.

Accordingly, we packed adequate food, water and provisions to comfortably reach Nik's hamlet in the *red colour country*, Isthad. I helped Kit build two four-wheeled carts with the supple and easy to use *bem* wood. In addition to carrying the necessities, the carts could also sit the kids if and when they got tired. We could not carry all the stone-tablets that Kit had recovered. So, Kit carefully selected a few of those that had critically important inscriptions on them. We put the remaining tablets in a room in my hut to preserve and protect those from the effects of the elements.

Thus, one fine evening, we started our journey towards the west in the soothing light of *Tin*. It's amazing, how we get attached to our surroundings. The humble hamlet had witnessed the beginning of a new life together for Kit and Ket. Their children, Sook and Soor were born and brought up in its lap. Until that point in time, the kids had never been beyond the areas surrounding the green pasture. Now, for the first time, they were to see the outside world, which they had only heard about.

We crossed a hillock at the western rim of the green pasture and soon lost sight of the hamlet at the eastern horizon behind us. Then the realities of the Violet Land took over our attention. Indeed, like a huge maze, it appeared to be the same in every direction. Many of the marks of the earlier trail had become obscure. Keeping the direction right in that terrain was almost impossible. It was easy to get lost in that maze. We depended entirely on Kit's ability to navigate through that mazy terrain.

We trekked during night and rested at day. At the morning of the fifteenth day, for the first time, I saw *Let* in its red manifestation. Everything appeared reddish in that predominantly red light. We were relieved and happy to have reached Isthad. Kit said to me, "Doctor, this is my *colour country* of birth."

For fourteen days we had been practically walking and resting under the open sky. It was getting hard on the kids. We wanted to reach the shelter of Nik's hamlet early. So, on that day, after resting for a while we continued our journey a bit towards the north, as directed by Kit.

We reached Nik's hamlet by afternoon. From a distance, the hamlet looked exactly like Kit had described it in his diary; a dozen minimalistic huts among a few trees with lanes in between. It had striking resemblance with our own hamlet in the Violet Land. I recalled that both the hamlets were built by the same folk.

I could imagine that Nik's hamlet would be full of activity of the rural folk who lived there. The males would take their herd of domesticated animals, the *bovs,* to the pastures and cultivate the surrounding lands. The domestic chores would mainly be done by the females. Their children would merrily play in the open and grow up in the lap of nature. They would sell their surplus produce in the nearby town and buy their provisions from there.

But, as we approached the hamlet, it became gradually clear to us that the hamlet was a deserted place now. The huts looked unkempt and a few of those, which were towards the Violet Land, were in a somewhat dilapidated state. Kit told us, "These huts must have been damaged by the harsh winds that blow from the Violet Land."

He led us through the lanes and stopped before a small hut facing south located at the western part of the hamlet. He paused and took a closer look at the low entrance door of the hut.

"This must be Nik's hut," guessed Ket.

Kit slowly turned to her, nodded and said, "Let's check it out."

It was apparent that the hut was unoccupied. Still, Kit knocked at the entrance door. As expected, no one answered to the knock. Then, Kit gently pushed the door. The door was ajar and readily gave way with a shrill sound of the hinge. One by one, we followed Kit and stepped onto the dusty floor inside the hut. Inside, we found Nik's cot, his armchair and a few other household articles. From their condition it was clear that no one had used those for years. As we were contemplating what to do next and where to go, Sook pointed out that there was something written in darker ink on the, now grey, wall above the cot. It read, *Meet me at Neoton four kilometres north-west from here- Nik.*

It took us another hour to reach Neoton. A Hoola hour is longer than an hour on Earth. By then *Let* was approaching the horizon and preparing to set. Neoton turned out to be quite a bustling city with all the amenities of a well-planned city life but everything was quite unlike anything I had ever seen anywhere on Earth. There were wide streets crossing each other at right angles, huge sky-scraping buildings and, most amazingly, strange looking cars quietly moving and even flying in every direction. I was agape with awe at the height of their technology. Sook and Soor were pretty amused too. This was the first time they came across a city. A few pedestrians, clad in their strange but stylish attires, curiously looked at our rather simplistic dresses and the primitive looking *bem* wood carts in which we were carrying our remaining provisions and the historic stone-tablets. As they came nearer, Kit asked them, "Could you please direct us to the residence of Nik, the wise? That is how his folks called him."

The youngsters among the group burst into laughter.

"What's so amusing?" firmly enquired Ket.

Then an elderly Hoo came forward and said, "You seem to be coming from some remote place. This is a city of hundreds of thousands. There may be hundreds of Niks, wise or fool, living here. How can we guide you if you do not have the complete address?"

Thus the group went away. We realised the problem we were in. It was like trying to find a needle in a haystack. *Let* was about to set. We were exhausted and needed a shelter to spend the night. We desperately looked for any civic office for help. We passed by a few more blocks. Then, a miracle happened. Before we noticed it, a gorgeous looking car came from the opposite direction and pulled up by us. Two Hoo boys in their late teens came out of the car. They were neatly dressed in red stripped uniforms and held learning gadgets in their hands. Apparently, they were returning home from their school. The boys jubilantly came towards Kit. At first, Kit did not understand what they were up to. Then, one of the teens said to him, "We noticed you from a distance as you looked like the people of our old hamlet. Coming nearer we recognised you, Kit. Do you remember, when we were kids, we lived at the green pasture in the Violet Land? You brought us back to Isthad."

"Who are you? How do you know my name?" exclaimed Kit.

Now the other teen said, "Don't you remember, you told us fabulous stories and sometimes played with us? I am Pin."

Then the former teen said, "I am Fin."

Hearing this, Kit joyously said, "O Pin, hey Fin, you have grown up so much. I could not recognise you." Then he introduced us to the teens and said to them, "We have come all the way from the green pasture to see you and meet Nik, the wise."

"Nik, the wise, and his brother, Mik, are the heads of Neoton now," said Pin.

Thereafter, the teens made a few conversations over their audio-video wrist gadgets and quickly arranged a couple of cars for us. We abandoned the carts and boarded the cars along with our belongings and the stone-tablets. Nik and Mik warmly welcomed us in their lush official apartment in the 72nd floor of a hundred storey building in the central business district of Neoton. They were quite aged and looked identical with long white beards but hardly any hair on their hemispherical heads. They were about five and a half feet tall and wrinkled-faced. There was nostalgia galore. Nik said, "I always hoped that you would come back one day. That is why I wrote those words on the wall of my hut. Thanks to Istha that, now you are back."

Kit thanked them for the welcome and said, "It would be better if you had written your full address there. I did not know that you are the heads here. But for the chanced meeting with Pin and Fin, it would be very difficult to find you here. It's amazing to see that they easily recognised me."

"I was advised not to write the full address due to security reasons," Nik explained and said, "Your admirers are pandemic in Isthad and abroad. Every one of the old hamlet has your photograph."

Then, Kit introduced us to them. They were surprised to meet Ket, Isthadian Kit's Inthadian wife, and their kids, Sook and Soor. But their surprise knew no bounds when they were told that, I am an Earthling. Nevertheless, they happily and readily greeted us.

Now, Kit showed them the stone-tablets and said, "We have brought in a crucial piece of Isthad-Inthad history; something that has the potential to change the very way these two *colour countries* perceive each other. I shall tell you the details later."

"This *colour conflict* between the two *colour countries* is still a menace though the younger generation is less likely to buy it," opined Nik, the wise.

Then, Kit asked them, "How are my parents? How is my teacher, Z and how are my friends?"

Mik replied, "They are all right. They miss you a lot. But they are sad at the malice that some Isthadians throw at you for losing the Sword to the Inthadians."

"The *Sword of Istha* belongs to Isthad. Isthad must get back the Sword," affirmed Kit.

10

THE SWORD OF ISTHA

Isth, the Originator of the red *colour* and the founder of the red *colour* country, Isthad, had achieved many legendary feats during his lifetime. One of his amazing feats was the creation of the *Sword of Istha* for the protection of the *red colour* and of Isthad. The best available technology of his time was employed to make the Sword. Its blade was made with a gleaming red metal specially devised for the purpose. Followers of Isth contributed precious stones and gems, which were decoratively embellished on the handle of the Sword. Then Isth initiated the Sword by chanting the sacred verses of Istha. It remained in his possession till his death. Thus the awesome eternal quality of Istha was imbued into the Sword through the purity of Isth.

Thereafter, the Sword had been carefully wrapped in red velvet and preserved in an intricately decorated *bem*-wood chest. Over millennia, the Isthadians cherished the Sword as a sacred symbol of the authority of their red deity, Istha. In the hands of a pure Isthadian the Sword spewed fire and had tremendous physical powers. Its very presence played havoc with the enemy's confidence.

The Sword, however, had a curse attached to it. If any impure Hoo touched the Sword, he would incur the wrath of Istha. In reality, it remained chiefly as a symbol of the power of Istha. Hardly anyone touched it. The *bem*-wood chest was opened from time to time on important occasions.

The physical powers of this most important Isthadian object had to be summoned in order to fend off a fierce invasion on Isthad by the Inthadians. As the General of the Isthadian army, Kit had raised the Sword and, with his army, pushed the Inthadian soldiers back to their territory. But, he was wounded and captured along with the Sword by the Inthadians. Subsequently, he had managed to escape from captivity with the help of Ket, his beloved. But the Sword had remained with the Inthadians. Kit's opponents in his home country maligned him by indicating that he had given away the Sword to the Inthadians. All these incidents happened before Kit's visit to Earth.

Now, to erase this malice off his face, Kit must get back the Sword from the Inthadians.

Meanwhile, the Inthadians faced a few problems in trying to shift the Sword from near the Isthad-Inthad border to their capital, Ethena. Firstly, the gray side of the personality of anyone who touched the Sword became exposed. Such was the supernatural quality of the Sword. So, the Inthadian soldiers generally became reluctant and refrained from holding It. No one likes its grey side to be exposed. Secondly, even the rare Inthadians who managed to lift the Sword could not unleash its full powers. The Sword moved awkwardly in their hands injuring themselves.

Then they tried to destroy the Sword. But all their efforts went in vein. The Sword easily cut through the heavy metal equipment with which they tried to crush it. In spite of their technological advances, they could not find out the key to the Sword's legendary powers.

The Inthadian rulers decided against bringing such a hazardous weapon to their capital endangering their citizens. Instead, they commissioned a fortified building at a secret location near the border and put the Sword in it under all-time surveillance. They declared a grand and fitting reward to anyone who could help them to unlock the secrets of the *Sword of Istha*.

Now, Kit solemnly told Nik, the wise, "I will get the Sword."

The crinkled eyed elderly Hoo looked at Kit's eyes and worriedly said, "Going by your past feats, I do not doubt your capabilities. By the look of your eyes it is apparent that you have already made up your mind. Still, I would like you to consider the heavy odds that are against you."

Taking a cue from Nik, Ket anxiously said, "Don't you remember dear, you escaped from your captivity in Inthad? If you go there, they will surely put you behind the bars again. We have already spent many years in separation. How will I raise the kids without you?"

Kit caressed her shoulder and assured her, "Don't worry sweetheart, I have a plan. I will be all right. You will be safe here. I will be back soon. Before I meet my parents and my teacher, Z, I must bring the Sword back." Still directing his gaze on his family, he said to Nik, "Sir, please take care of my family and my friend." He looked at me and continued, "Doctor looked after me very well while I was on Earth. Now he is our honoured guest to Hoola."

"Remember what I told you after you reunited my folks with me. Consider this place to be your home. Your near ones are dear to us. Your friend is our friend," said Nik.

I interrupted saying, "I feel quite at home here. I shall be all right. You take care of yourself, Kit. We shall be waiting for you."

Indeed, the elderly brothers made every effort to make our stay comfortable with adequate food, trendy cloths, luxurious accommodations and even audio-video wrist gadgets for long distance communications.

Thereafter, Kit bade us farewell and left *Neoton,* with some food, water and money, towards the Isthad-Inthad border. At that juncture, we did not know whether we would see him again.

Kit, however, did come back after a couple of weeks and told us his awesome story.

11

VENTURE TO INTHAD

After leaving us at *Neoton,* Kit headed straight to the border and spent three days there before entering the *blue colour country*, Inthad. During these three days, he earnestly took refuge in the blue deity, Intha, and His blue *colour*. By the end of the third day, he was completely transformed into an Inthadian. Not only his long furry tail but his entire being became *blue*.

Thus he sneaked into Inthad as an Inthadian. His goal was to reach Ethena, the capital of Inthad. After reaching the nearest Inthadian town to the border, he boarded a public car for Ethena. On his way, he saw new places and met a few Inthadians and his co-passengers. Through these interactions, he found that many things had changed in Inthad since he had escaped from there. Most strikingly, the younger generation of Inthadians was not willing to carry on the divisive egoistic baggage of the older block. The new generation wanted to live and enjoy their lives. They wanted peace, development and prosperity rather than war, bloodshed and death.

After reaching Ethena, Kit called on the *public liaison officer* to the *colour rulers* of Inthad, at her office. He politely said to the elderly Inthadian lady, "Madam,

I am Tik. Is the offer for the reward on the *Sword of Istha* still on?"

The liaison officer raised her eyebrows and squarely enquired, "Why? You want to give it a try? You want to earn some quick bucks? Do you think it is that easy?"

Kit kept his composure and calmly replied, "I know how to fight with that Sword."

"What makes you so confident?" asked the officer.

Kit said, "For many years, I have lived among the Isthadians in Isthad. I know their ways. I am sure I can do it."

Now, the officer toned down a bit and said, "Look, so far only five persons have responded to the announcement of the reward. One of those got separated from his wife as his unfaithfulness became exposed by the Sword. Another one is still languishing in rehabilitation on charges of theft. The remaining three were severely injured by the Sword and had to be hospitalised. In the last three years, no one else has come forward. You are the sixth one. You will have to convince the rulers and seek their permission before you can make the attempt. I can fix a meeting with the rulers if you still insist."

Kit nodded, thanked the officer and went back to his rented accommodation in the outskirts of Ethena. After a couple of days he received a call on his wrist gadget from the liaison officer. The meeting with the *colour rulers* of Inthad had been fixed on that afternoon at the Dome, the place from where Inthad was ruled. Accordingly Kit presented himself at the gate of the Dome, sharp on time. As usual, he was ushered through the corridors to the main hall of the Dome. As he walked through the middle passage of the hall, the Inthadians sitting on both sides of the passage curiously turned towards him. After all, it was after years that someone had sought to make an attempt at the significant Sword. The *colour rulers* of Inthad, gracefully dressed in their traditional blue outfits, were seated on a finely designed blue podium at the end of the hall, in front of Kit. He saw new younger faces among the *colour rulers* than the ones he had met years ago when he had been captive in Inthad.

Kit was asked to approach the podium. Kit serenely bowed to the rulers and stood before them. One of the rulers asked him, "Well Mr. Tik, we found no record of you in our registers. Could you tell us why?"

"For generations, my ancestors have been living in Isthad. I was also born and brought up in Isthad. All my records are there. Anyway, I guess, my capability will be enough proof of my credential," Kit replied confidently.

Another ruler asked, "What proof do you have in support of your claim? What guarantee do you have that you will not waste our precious time?"

Kit patiently said, "I understand you have the cosmetic technology to change the form of a red Isthadian into a blue Inthadian?"

"That's true," said the ruler.

"I can bring about a deeper transformation automatically without any artificial means. If you give me three days' time, I shall come back in the red Isthadian form," said Kit.

Now, the rulers seemed a bit skeptic. Even so, solving the riddle of the Sword had been a serious pending issue for them. The Chairperson of the *colour rulers* of Inthad declared, "We give you three days' time. If you come back in the Isthadian form, you will be given a chance to decode the secret of the Sword. Otherwise, you will be penalised for making false claims before the rulers."

Kit thanked the rulers and went back to his temporary rented residence. Thereafter, he locked himself up in a room. For the next three days he continuously aligned and submitted himself to the red deity, Istha. Three days later, he came out of his room, fully transformed into an Isthadian, from inside out. His tail had turned into gorgeous red. His entire being exuded a reddish aura.

The new *colour rulers* of Inthad could hardly believe their eyes when they saw that the blue Inthadian had indeed transformed into an apparently authentic Isthadian within a matter of three days. They had never heard anything like this before that point in time, less seen. Still, they insisted on a medical test of Kit to ensure that his appearance was not a trick of visual illusion. Kit was taken to a sophisticated hospital in Ethena where a team of Inthadian doctors performed a series of tests and examinations on him, particularly his, now red, tail. The medical reports startlingly confirmed that presently Kit was a thorough Isthadian. His appearance was not shallow. He was red from inside out.

As astonished as they were, the *colour rulers* of Inthad fixed the following morning for Kit's attempt at the reward on the Sword. The rulers had deferred the day of the attempt by a day so that they themselves could take the time off their busy schedule and witness Kit's attempt. By now, they had started taking Kit seriously.

On that eventful day, Kit reported at the Dome early in the morning, as per the schedule. He was provided with a flying car. The *colour rulers* of Inthad boarded their official flying cars. They were accompanied by an elaborate array of convoys, ranks of the Inthadian military and a team of paramedics. The convoy headed straight to the secret location near the border where the Sword was preserved in a specially constructed building.

They reached the border in an hour and landed near the secret building. The soldiers guarding the fortified building opened the gate and the convoy walked into the spacious chamber in which the Sword was housed. The *colour rulers* took their seats flanked by their delegates and senior military officers. Without much formality they gave their nod to Kit to make his attempt. Kit thanked the rulers and proceeded to the Sword, which was placed in a glass showcase. Two soldiers gently opened the lid of the showcase and then stepped back. Some of the spectators who witnessed Kit's display on that day subsequently described it thus.

First, Kit aligned himself and his long, luxuriant furry red tail to the Sword. He recited a sacred verse dedicated to the red deity, Istha. Then he gracefully picked up the Sword from its resting place and held it by the handle, with both his hands stretched before himself. The red metal blade of the Sword shone; as if it had been awakened. Kit started with a few gyrating movements of his body and slow swings of the Sword. Gradually his movements became more rapid.

Then he performed the rhythmic, elegant and delicate movements of the war-dance of the ancient and the eternal Istha. Suddenly his being was transformed into a ball of fire. Now his fierce movements were faster than the eyes could follow. His long and agile tail majestically slashed through the air in unison with his dance like a serpentine whip. The Sword seemed like an extension of his own body. His face looked intense and he seemed to be utterly aware and in control of each and every movement. In spite of the intensity, his eyes looked calm and in a state of trance. The Sword of Istha, in his hands, swung and swerved through the air spewing thunderous sparks. After dancing like that for about half an hour, Kit beautifully concluded the dance with a final movement of the Sword, finely slashing through a two feet wide stone column. Then he formally bowed to his spectators.

Everyone present in the chamber, stood up in awe. The *colour rulers* of Inthad congratulated him for his successful attempt at the Sword and assured him of the promised prize. The *General* of the Inthadian army enquired of Kit, "Was it war technique or artistic dance? I have studied all the war techniques. There is no record of such a war-dance anywhere on Hoola. Where did you learn to fight like that?"

Kit serenely replied, "It is a merger of both fight and dance; of elegance and lethal accuracy. By the grace of Istha, I learnt it by *thought exercises,* directly from Istha Himself."

None, including the *General,* had expected such a reply. They could hardly believe Kit's words. But, then they could not disbelieve their own eyes either. They remained astonished. The Chairperson said, "All you have to do now is to reveal the secret of the Sword and then you can claim your reward."

Kit said, "There is more to this than meets the eyes. Perhaps you have discovered by now that this is easier said than done. What I shall tell you now may sound unusual or even irrational.

"In simple words, the key to the firing power of the Sword is this: seeing the red deity, Istha, everywhere, in everything and in everybody. While swinging the Sword in the air or striking an object or an opponent enemy with it, the bearer of the Sword must perceive Istha in each of these, the air, the object and the enemy. Only a pure Hoo of the Isthadian order can realise such a vision after many years of alignments and prayers to Istha. The all-pervading Istha draws the fire out the Sword from within the air or the struck object or the enemy. To control the Sword, the bearer must first control its own self. The Sword must be used with controlled balance and stability; not with raw hatred. The reason why the enemy is fighting you may be as great as the cause that compels you to fight. Realising thus, the fighter has to unselfishly perform his duty without expecting anything in return.

"However, this Sword is so constituted that it can only be used for the defence of Isthad and can never be used against the Isthadians.

"Allow me to mention here that, all *colours* lead to the same Supreme Being. Because, the entire relative *colour* manifestations emerge from the singularity of the Absolute Truth of the Supreme. Therefore, every Hoo is potent to manifest any *colour* it likes. Of course, purity and perseverance are required."

Everyone heard Kit with rapt attention. His expressions, body-language, gestures and delivery exuded the depth of his truth and his profound realisation behind every word that he spoke. It turned out to be an eye opener for the Inthadians. They usually belittled the Isthadian's stress on devotion and love as irrational. They boasted of their intellectual orientation, their technological advancement and the higher frequency of their *blue* light than that of the Isthadian *red*. Now, they saw that they had something to learn from the Isthadians. Kit's practical display and profound discourse readily appealed to the truth seeking psyche of the Inthadians. Their interest in learning about the Sword extended to queries about the Isthadian *colour* culture.

After a few whispers among the rulers, the Chairperson declared, "You may claim your reward now. We will do our best to keep our word."

Without any hesitation Kit said, "Please return the Sword to the Isthadians. This will go a long way in improving your relations with them."

The rulers smiled. One of the rulers said, "We will consider that. Do you want anything more?"

Now, Kit divulged, "Four days back you met Tik, a true blue Inthadian, one of the facets of my multi-potency. Now, standing before you is Kit, the red Isthadian, your absconding war-prisoner."

Rather than being surprised, the rulers seemed to be pleased to hear that. One of them said, "We already know that you are Kit. It was absurd that we did not have any record of Tik in our registers. So we were suspicious. Yesterday, during your medical tests you matched our biometric records of Kit. We found it intriguing. We could have crossed you then and there. But we decided to wait and watch your movements to find out your real motives.

"Sometime after you managed to escape, the news of your escape was leaked. The fact that our own arrow struck one of our own, Doctor Ket, pained everyone in spite of the fact that she helped you to escape. There were many protests against the manner in which the matter was handled. You were our war-prisoner and not a criminal.

Since then a lot of changes have taken place here, particularly, how we treat the war-prisoners. Accordingly, your name has been struck off our absconding prisoner's list five years after you escaped. So far as we are concerned, you are free since then. You do not seem to know that. But still you entered into Inthad risking imprisonment. Why, only for this Sword?"

Kit felt relieved. He said, "Do not be worried about Ket. By the grace of the Supreme, she has been resurrected. We have united and have two lovely kids. They are safely in Isthad now."

The Inthadians were pleasantly surprised. "They are welcome here. This is their country. Where have you been all these years? You seem to be as young as you were then," asked a ruler.

To their utter surprise, Kit said, "I have been to several places, including to another planet called Earth, millions of light years away from here. There, people do not grow tails."

"That's incredible," said one delegate.

"But true. Doctor Adam Smith, my friend from Earth, has come to Hoola with me. He is also in Isthad now," said Kit. He further declared, "At the right occasion I shall tell you and all even more incredible things about our own histories that may change the very way we see each other. Till then, please brace up to hear the unheard truth. Truth, which had been buried under the sands in the Violet Land for thousands of years, has been dug up and deciphered. We have found out how two great individual's mutual dislike is responsible for giving rise to this millennia old unwholesome rivalry between Inthad and Isthad. You will know then, how our seeds of sorrow were sown at the very genesis of our *colours*."

Now, no one doubted his words. Kit's wisdom had opened up the mindset of the Inthadian rulers. They saw that they had no direct use of the *Sword of Istha* and the Inthadians could not use the Sword without Kit's help. So they decided to hand it over to Kit as his promised reward.

Thus, Kit not only retrieved the Sword from the Inthadians without spilling a drop of blood, but, more importantly, he opened up the Inthadian heart towards the Isthadians. The Isthadian grudge over the Inthadians was subdued to a great extent after the latter returned the Sword to them. Kit achieved a friendlier atmosphere between the two belligerent *colour countries;* something that had eluded them with many years of animosity and war. Now, he happily met his parents and his mentor, Z.

At first, Isthadian Kit's union with Inthadian Ket seemed to be too radical to Kit's aging parents' exclusive reliance on the *red colour.* But, the moment they saw their lovely grandchildren, Sook and Soor, all their reservations evaporated like camphor in a pan. Z was ecstatic to receive his prodigy and readily approved Kit's union to his other outstanding student, Ket. As the Principal of the international boarding school in the city of Aton in Isthad, Z had known them since they were about eight years of age. He was the only one who had tacitly understood the depth of their mutual affection even at their early age of fourteen.

Kit, once again, became a national hero in Isthad and immensely popular in Inthad as well. Not only that, the stories of his extraordinary feats and his visit to Earth spread all over Hoola and soon he became a living legend catching the imagination of the global populations.

12

IBEN

Eventually, Kit invited the rulers of both Isthad and Inthad for a face to face dialogue in an attempt to bring their mutual animosity to an end. He volunteered to mediate in the dialogue. The ceaseless war had been costing these two great nations dear. There was economic urgency to at least ease the war. Besides, the newer generations had grown increasingly averse to carry on the burden of the egoistic baggage of their ancestors. They wanted peace and development more than anything else. Under these compulsive circumstances, the relatively orthodox rulers of Isthad and Inthad reluctantly decided to give the dialogue a go.

The *blue* and the *red colour rulers* agreed to hold the deliberation at the auditorium of the prestigious international school at the city of Aton in Isthad. This auditorium is not only huge but also equipped with the state of the art interiors, gadgets and decorations necessary to host an assembly of such grandeur and gravity.

I recalled that, Kit had written in his diary that he had studied in this school. It is here that he had metamorphosed from being a naïve rural boy into one of the most promising adults on the planet, Hoola, under the able guidance of his mentor, the then Principal of the school, Z.

Now, on the day of the proposed convention, the delegates from the rulers of both the *colour countries* sat on the stage. Kit, along with a few of his fellows, also sat on the stage. Intellects, dignitaries, distinguished guests and laities from both the *colour countries* sat among the audience, Inthadians on the right and Isthadians on the left. There were interest and eager anticipation on both sides. At stake was a possible mitigation of their differences and an amicable solution for peaceful coexistence.

After brief introduction and formalities, the delegates of the *red* and the *blue colour rulers* took the stage one by one. They were eloquent and diplomatic in their delivery but each wasted little time in trying to tacitly assert their supremacy over the other.

Each side claimed that the Originator of their *colour* was the only son of Iben whom he took along with him for a significant sacrifice. Thus each of the two *colours* claimed exclusive lineage to Iben, the great. Not only that, a few of them opined that, their Deity was the original Deity of Iben whom he had neither named nor described. Some of them were of the view that the sacrifice took place within their geographical territory. The competition on the stage readily percolated among the audience. Soon, the audience became embroiled in a hue and cry over the exclusive credit for the great sacrifice that Iben had earnestly intended and almost committed.

In this doldrums and uproar among the audience, Kit gently rose from his seat on the stage and quietly approached the centre of the stage. Someone from the audience immediately noticed him and shouted, "Look, here comes Kit."

There was a delightful aura of such peace and serenity around him that the cacophony of the audience gradually toned down to murmur and then to whispers. By the time Kit reached the centre of the stage, there was complete silence. Every ear was eager to hear what would be delivered from his lips.

Then, with the conviction of the skyscraping mountains, Kit said in his beautiful resonating voice, "My ladies and my lords, I salute thee the way I salute the Supreme Almighty." Thus he aligned himself to the audiences. First he turned to the Inthadians and his white tail turned into blue. Then he turned to the Isthadians and his tail turned red. Thus Kit physically demonstrated that *red* and *blue* are non-dual, being two states of the same Hoo entity.

The silence of the audience was spontaneously broken by a rapturous applause that continued for a couple of minutes. Then Kit continued, "The Supreme is the singular source of everything in this universe. The Supreme is our Father, our Mother and our Creator. I perceive the essence of the Supreme in each one of you."

Saying thus, Kit went on to reveal the stone-tablets to both the *colour communities* and articulated the truths that were inscribed on those as follows:

"During his time, Iben achieved many astonishing feats but the following is the one feat that is mainly responsible for securing him permanence in the Hoo legends.

"The stone-tablets tell that, thousands of years ago, there was a fertile land in what is now known as the *Forbidden Violet Land.* A community of ancient people thrived there. Iben was the most pious among the community. He realised great wisdoms from the premises of his devotion to his Deity whom he never named nor described. Some Hoo scholars speculate that it was a Violet Deity though there is no evidence to support this opinion.

"Iben had two sons named Inth and Isth. As wise as he was, Iben never imposed his wisdoms upon his beloved sons. Instead, he simply made his realisations available to them and allowed them to spontaneously absorb their essence. His extraordinarily gifted sons imbibed the richness of his wisdoms but they did not stop there. Following their respective individual inclinations, they themselves further evolved their own wisdoms in the light of their own realisations. Legends also have it that these two immensely talented brothers were quite out of tune with each other. In certain respect one seemed exactly like the opposite of the other. Their discord was most prominent in their contradicting approaches to wisdom and spirituality.

"One night, their father, Iben, had a vision of his Deity. In order to test Iben's faith in It, the Deity asked Iben to sacrifice his beloved sons. The next morning, Iben woke up early and called his sons and told them about his vision. The two worthy sons of Iben readily agreed to sacrifice themselves without asking any question.

"Thus the three of them bathed in what is now the dried up Forbidden River. Then they made the gruelling climb to the peak of the mountain that is now called the Forbidden Mountain. After reaching the peak, Iben embraced his sons one by one for the last time. Then he lined up the sons at the edge of the cliff with their backs towards him. Thereafter, showing no hesitation to execute his Deity's mandate, Iben pushed his dear sons off the cliff into the deep gorge.

"Pleased with the sacrifices, the Deity immediately transformed the sons into two identical soothing white dove-like, but alien, birds. Their only difference was in their eyes. While Inth had deep blue eyes, Isth developed scarlet ones. The Deity said to Iben, 'Dear Iben, don't be worried. Your sons will regain their Hoo forms as soon as they touch the ground. Your sacrifice shall be remembered with reverence through the ages. My unceasing blessings remain with you.'

"But, for some reason only known to them, the two sons did not go back to their father, Iben. True to their contrasting inclinations, they flew off in opposite directions. Inth headed east while Isth flew westwards.

"After flying for days, weeks and months, the two brothers landed on two distant lands and got back to their Hoo forms. Inth landed in a place where the daylight is blue. He was a great intellectual. He employed his intellect and, through fine analysis, revealed the subtle and superb realities of and about the existence of the universe. Eventually, he realised the Supreme Unity in the form of a blue Deity whom he called Intha, which, in the Hoo language, means the *Lord of Inth*. His sacrosanct tail turned *blue*. The Hoos who followed him also developed brilliant blue tails. Thus Inth became the Originator of the *blue colour*.

"Isth, on the other hand, reached a land where the daylight is red. His gift was in his heart. Through years of unselfish sublime devotional services, he emptied and opened up his heart to the Supreme. Gradually, the emptiness of his heart was filled with the Supreme Inspiration. From that Inspiration oozed spontaneous knowledge, even though Isth never sought after knowledge. He realised the Supreme in the form of a red Deity whom he called Istha. Like him, his followers also developed radiant red tails.

"Mysteriously enough, none of the two brothers ever went back to their father, Iben, in the land of their birth where the daylight is violet. They even forbade their respective followers to visit the Violet land. Neither of them ever spoke about the other brother. So, for millennia, each of their respective followers thought that Iben had only one son and the Originator of their *colour* was that son. Some Hoo scholars opine that the brothers avoided each other and their father to maintain the distinctiveness of their respective approaches to the Absolute Truth. However there are oppositions to such views.

"Over the next few centuries, the land of their birth became totally abandoned and came to be known as the Forbidden Violet Land. The mountain cliff, from where they were pushed off by their father, was later called the Forbidden Mountain. The river at the foot of the mountain, in which they had bathed on the day of the sacrifice, has long dried up exposing the spear-shaped crystal stones of the river bed. But even now it is called a river, the Forbidden River.

"Meanwhile, the *colour wisdoms* of Inth and Isth spread over vast land masses on either side of the Forbidden Violet Land. Their *colours* were passed on from one generation to another. Thus two great *colour countries* grew up. The country on the western side of the Violet Land, where the daylight is red, was called Isthad, meaning the land of Istha or the red country.

Similarly, the country on the eastern side of the Violet Land, where the day light is blue, came to be known as Inthad.

"Over thousands of years since the ancient times of Inth and Isth, the underlying wisdoms of their *colours* have mostly faded away from the public consciousness. Today, for most of the Hoos, the *colours* remain merely as a stereotyped traditional identity and an external appearance. These *colour identities* have become so rigid that a formidable gulf has been wedged between the two *colours* due to their apparent outward differences. Today, the two people are grappling to come to terms with the menace of this *colour conflict*.

"Thus, a single *sibling-rivalry*, between Iben's two great sons, Inth and Isth, snow-balled into unabated animosity between the two great *colour countries* and resulted in unparalleled mayhem and bloodshed. Even the common paternity of the Originators of the two *colours* has been easily forgotten. Astonishingly, the two *colour communities*, in spite of being in such close proximity demarcated by a thin borderline for as long as millennia, remained separated by their *colour differences*, oblivious of the common ancestry of their Originators. Only if the two peoples could wake up to this reality of their brotherhood/sisterhood, the underlying singular Unity behind the two *colours* could be realised and the gulf between the two *colour countries* be bridged, half of the seven billion strong global Hoo population on Hoola would be unified.

"Now, the wise readily realises the fact that, the real essence, the crux, the centre and the moral of Iben's great sacrifice rest in the depth of his devotion and in the height of his submission to his Deity and not so much in whom he took for the sacrifice. This has gone into oblivion. Instead, each of the two *colour communities* thinks that some credit is associated with being prepared for the sacrifice and is merely bent on taking the credit for the sacrifice. Has there ever been any dearth of people who covet credit? What is there in that dull and mundane credit taking? How does it benefit us, the Hoos? What else do we gain from it other than the endless animosity that it has evoked between the two *colour countries*?" Kit solemnly enquired.

None uttered a word. Kit continued, "At any given point in time, we find our-selves positioned in the *present*, which stands between the *past* and the *future*.

"*Past* is something which has gone by. No matter how hard we may try, the clock cannot be run backwards. The incidents, which have already happened, cannot be changed. However, the impressions of the *past* linger on and cannot be dismantled easily. Thus, traditions and conventions come into being. These things have their utilities and benefits but problems arise when these have outlived their time. Some traditions seem to hold on to our mind even long after those have become dysfunctional. Such perpetuation of outdated traditions often leads to agony and misery. Nevertheless, the educative value of the *past* cannot be underestimated. With this enriching legacy from the *past*, we have to move into the *future*, which is exactly the opposite of the *past*.

"Unlike the *past*, the *future* is mostly unknown and there is always an element of uncertainty about it. These aspects make the *future* fascinating and interesting and give birth to conjectures, speculations and predictions. If the *cause and effect* patterns of history are extrapolated forward, we may have a somewhat hazy gaze into the future.

Moreover, as Hoo beings, we do have certain control over our future. In order to exercise that control, we must first control our own internal nature. There may be a multitude of methods and ways of doing so and raising our consciousness to the higher planes of truth, wisdom, selflessness and bliss. Once we are able to reach the purity of these higher planes, our minds can perceive the *light of vision.* With this *light of vision*, we can guide and propel ourselves into that glorious future when the heavens will descend on Hoola and we, the one Hoo race, will live with our inherent divinity manifested. That is the highest goal and the ultimate destiny of the race.

"Obviously, all these good works have to be done in this wonderful time that we call the *present,* which is the bridge between our *past* and our *future*. Therefore, the significance of the *present* is immense and it is the most important of the three parts of time. Let us derive the most out of this *present*."

Kit paused and went on to say, "My ladies and my lords, the task at our hand is not easy. Habits created over millennia are not easy to undo. For many generations now, the Hoo psyche of the two *colours* has been veiled by these illusions. Particularly in this case, the basic *recognition zeal* has thoroughly overwhelmed the reality. Knowing the truth is not enough. What lay ahead of us, is to understand it and to accept it. Then, we shall have to realise the truth in our inner selves and manifest that realisation from inside out into the external environment. With the right knowledge and education, we can reach the goal in as early as three generations; if we start now, that is."

13 THE NEW NATION

The Violet Land was not a part of any other *colour country* as traditionally it was considered to be forbidden to go there. Most of the people who had dared to go there got lost in that hypnotic natural maze and lost their lives. Kit was the only one who could decode the secrets of the land and navigate through it. Most of the land was unknown and uncharted. Kit declared ownership of this Violet Land unto him and offered to share it with the Hoos who would like to come and settle there and work with him for the cause of the *psychic harmony of the Hoo race*. This was a very bold and over-optimistic step. At the time of this declaration, it seemed that no one would be interested to come to the barren terrains of the Violet Land and bear its harsh elements leaving behind the hospitable living in their respective *colour countries*.

Within months of the declaration though, the foresightedness of Kit became evident. There were individuals among the Hoos who did not live off material resources alone. Their existence was not merely in pampering their bodies and entertaining their minds. They wanted to live for a cause and were willing to take up the hardships for that cause. Many of these Hoos – farmers, labourers, intellects, scholars, technologists, doctors, teachers, students, laities, male, female, old folk and youngsters from many *colour countries*, responded to Kit's offer and landed in the Violet Land. Kit fondly addressed them as the '*special ones*' and warmly welcomed each one of them.

The immigrants, who came to the Violet Land in search of the light that had shone through Kit, did not come empty handed. They brought along with them diversity of knowledge, expertise and their own Hoo talents and resourcefulness. They also had their friends and connections all over Hoola. Their settlements started from the hamlet at the green patch and gradually spread in all directions. Mere cultivation of the fields at the green patch around the hamlet could in no way sustain such a large settlement. Kit, more than anyone else, knew it better. He had already chalked out his plan for sustenance of the settlement.

As I have written before, technologically, the Hoos are a much advanced race than the humans. But, the downside of their technology is that they consume astounding amounts of energy. To generate this energy, they create tiny stars in their advanced power plants. One of the essential ingredients for the generation of power on this power-hungry planet is the marble shaped *dyne* stones.

I had read in Kit's diary that, it had been in the folklore since the ancient times that there are *dyne* stones in the Violet Land. In his youth, he made his first expedition to the hitherto unknown Violet Land in search of the precious stones for his native *red colour country*, Isthad. After years of hardship, a mine of *dyne* stones was discovered at a distance from the hamlet on the green patch.

Now, with the help of the immigrants, this mine was exploited. Later on a few more *dyne* stone rich mines were discovered elsewhere in the Violet Land. Soon, the nascent nation started minting money by exporting the stones to all over Hoola. With this money power they imported all the material resources that they required not only to survive but actually flourish in the Violet deserts. Thus, within a short span of a few years, a tiny but vibrant and spiritually and economically strong nation grew up there. They called this new nation Kithad, which, in the Hoo language, means *the land founded by Kit*. Our humble hamlet developed into a sprawling town. Kit named this town Hamton. Hamton became the capital of Kithad.

Most of the land was charted, roads were constructed and landmarks were put in place so no Kithadian would be lost in the maze of the Violet Land. However, they left the rim of the Violet Land around Kithad untouched to keep unauthorised intruders at bay. Any such Hoo would be lost in the maze of the Violet Land before it could reach Kithad. So no one would dare to breach this natural barrier.

Now, living in my own apartment in Hamton, I proudly looked back to those initial days when Kit and I were literally scavenging and did not know from where the next day's meal would come. Stranded in the hostile elements of the inhospitable land, we could hardly dream then that such a prosperous future awaited us and all those who subsequently came to settle there.

Notably, Kithad became the first multi-coloured country on Hoola. The people of this cosmopolitan nation were as multi-coloured as their planet Hoola itself; a heterogeneous demography. Though it grew on the Violet Land, Kithad remained spiritually white.

Everyone in Kithad was free to practice any *colour* of its own individual choice. Thus, *freedom of colour* came to existence on Hoola. The people happily embraced Kit's ideal of inclusiveness and accepted each other as they were. They chose Kit as their leader. Kit, a true multi-coloured personality, often wore white attire symbolising the assimilation of all the colours in him, instead of the traditional red apparels of his native *red colour country*, Isthad. Most of the time, his colour changing tail appeared white. It was a direct reflection of his boundless heart, which easily encompassed all.

Soon, a state of the art international university was opened at Hamton. The Hamton University had all the different faculties: arts, literature, science, economics and an elaborate *colour* faculty for the study and research into the essence and the natures of the three hundred odd *colours* and *colour shades* that existed on Hoola. Many exponents and scholars of the *colours* from all over Hoola joined the university. They wanted to see a new light of liberation through their respective *colours* but they did not have the necessary environment of openness for this in their respective home *colour countries*. New generation students enrolled at the university from all over the globe.

At the opening ceremony of the *colour* faculty, Kit addressed the assembly of the scholars and students and memorably outlined the aims of the faculty as follows:

"Revered scholars and promising students, I welcome you all to the Hamton University and thank you for coming here. As we know, presently the *colours* are fairly inseparable aspects of our Hoo being. Perhaps it is our *colours* that make us a unique race. I have been to planet Earth. There the human race does not have any *colour perception* and they do not develop *colour tails* like us.

Most probably, we have acquired these *colours* from the unique environments of our multi-coloured planet. It appears that, from the very beginning, consciously or sub-consciously, we were destined to be affected by our colourful environments.

"We are also aware that, our *colours* elevate our souls and yet, simultaneously fragment our Hoo race, most importantly, in our own psychologies. Why does this happen? We are here to attempt to open mindedly discover the details of the statics and the dynamics of our *colours* so that we may reach the crux of the problem and seek remedial solutions.

"Being among the multitude of diversity of *colours*, can the plight be to cling on to any one of them and then to say that, *that particular monochrome is supreme and it is all that there should be?* Yet, narrowed down by our respective rich but finite *colour traditions*, each Hoo tends to conceive its *colour* thus.

"Things, perspectives, perceptions and orientations change from individual to individual, from group to group, from community to community, from *colour country* to *colour country* and interestingly, at all these levels from time to time. In the process, we lose sight of our global existence due to our partial perceptions taken from our relative perspectives and diverse orientations.

"A possible remedy may be in double training our minds to revisit the global existence of the race as a whole from a universal perspective, rather than a narrowed down monochromatic one, to form an inclusive global perception while maintaining the *colour* choices, rather than the *colour* ascriptions, of the individual. Like, metal cuts metal and diamond cuts diamond, the partial divisive perceptions of each community have to be overridden by this, relatively new, inclusive global unifying perception with a spirit of accommodativeness and acceptance of each other."

Then, turning to the students Kit said, "Dear students, now I shall reveal a secret to you. '*Average*' or '*ordinariness*' is essentially a construction of the Hoo mind and therefore these have no existence in reality because, in the diversity of existence, each one is unique and thus extraordinary. The largely stereotyped and insensitive externality will hardly ever tell you how unique and how precious you are. That is something that you will have to find out yourself as no one else knows you better than you know yourself. Do not be afraid to look beyond the stereotypes in order to find your true Self. Even if you fail to find that *unique* and *extraordinary* 'You', it is always worth investing your time and energies in this quest. This is how your infinite potential can become manifest. *The goal of Hoo life is to realise, in this relative finiteness, the Absolute Infinite and thus, become free.*

"Hoo history is full of examples of ordinary Hoos who achieved extraordinary feats in their lives. Therefore, have faith in yourself.

"Now, when it comes to realisation of the Self, when it comes to that search for the Soul and when it comes to finding the Divine within, who else can be your best friend and philosopher than your own Self; only that Hoo who Itself is Self-realised and unselfish and is loving to you. Fortunate are those who find such a rare One as their teacher. For most Hoos, the search for such a One may continue for years and even lifetimes may go by in vein. Why wait, when you have a second option in your own Self. Who knows you, your thoughts, motives and aspirations more than your Self? The Self is ever present with you, your constant companion. You have perfect and direct communication with the Self without the need for any language, sign or symbol.

"The whole universe is set before you like a huge open book and a lifetime to gather knowledge. Defy the bandwagons. Step aside and witness everything external like a true student. Internally, be your own watchdog and notice the thoughts and their causes and effects. Most importantly, never lose sight of the wonderful and unique things that only you have thought. Focus and work on those and those will manifest. Thus serve all from inside out and realise the Self."

Kit paused and concluded his speech saying, "Please, preach not. If you can, serve all with your knowledge and wisdom without expecting anything in return. This way, ultimately you will gain the most. Because, then your knowledge will multiply and manifest and you will be nearer to the Divine than any amount of preaching activity can ever take you to.

"Serve all like a servant, perceiving the Divine in each. Then the Divine will manifest in you and in all those that receive your pure, undiluted knowledge; the heavens will descend upon Hoola.

"We have a wonderful opportunity to perform a great task for a grand purpose. The Supreme is ever with us."

The receptive audience remained in awe at the farsighted and iconoclastic optimism for the Hoo harmony that was exuded by Kit.

However, the divisive forces on Hoola were as active as the unifying ones. Sometime later, they would show their colours.

Where there is *good, evil* follows. *Selfishness shadows unselfishness.*

14
THE ABDUCTION

The marriage of Isthadian red Kit to Inthadian blue Ket had set a precedence of *inter-colour* marriage, which had broken the taboo on such marriages. Their children manifested that union. This inspired other youngsters who subsequently united thus. This fundamentally upset the *colour-differences*. It seemed like *colour harmony* would soon be a reality on Hoola. But it was not to be; not so soon, not so simply and not yet. A few hardened old-fashioned *colour rulers*, who gained from the *colour differences*, were infuriated. They saw that their exclusive control over their respective *colour communities* was losing ground threatening their positions of socio-economic and political advantages. These rulers had no reason to be happy about and to join these *inter-colour* marriage parties.

The physical conditions of the barren Violet Land, on which Kithad was established, had its inherent disadvantages. On this land, radio waves deviated unpredictably and posed serious problems not only in long-distance wireless communication via satellite but also to surveillance and security. To circumvent this problem, the nation was being wired and technological innovations were being sought. However, these measures were anything but adequate. Soon, this drawback would lead to grave consequences.

Just when Kithad was flourishing and things were going on well, the misfortune took place. One morning, to her horror, Ket found that Kit was missing. Everyone became alarmed. Later it turned out that one of Kit's bodyguards was also missing.

A couple of anxious days passed after Kit's sudden disappearance but neither Kit nor the guard could be found anywhere. On the third day, Sook became extremely retracted and calm. Since the morning, he refused to eat anything despite Ket's repeated attempts. We tried to console him by saying that we would do everything to find his father and that his father would come back soon, but he wouldn't even talk to anyone. He just sat at the window with his gaze firmly fixed at the southern horizon. Knowing his unrelenting nature, we decided to leave him to himself for a while. Ket, however, kept constant watch on her son despite her own worries. Strangely enough, the tip of Sook's tiny tail poked out of the window from time to time and directed in all directions like a serpent trying to sniff the air around it. Only after well past noon, Sook left his seat at the window, went to his mother and holding her hand uttered three words in the Hoo language, which mean, "Pa – south – tower."

His mother called me and others and asked, "What do you make of it?"

I had no clue whatsoever. I had very limited knowledge about Hoola. However, the *ruler* in charge of the foreign affairs of Kithad put together his guess within a few moments. He explained to Ket, "We have checked every part of Kithad but Kit has not been found. He is not in Kithad. Now, to the south, Kithad tapers into a common border between Isthad and Inthad. Further south is the *yellow colour country*, Hunthad."

"The *tower of Gumba.*" Ket interrupted impatiently.

"Yes, the famous tower at Gumba, the capital of Hunthad. That is what readily comes to mind. Sook seems to imply that Kit is in that tower!" exclaimed the ruler.

Ket immediately responded, "I am sure, Sook knows his intuitions."

"But we had no plans to send anybody there in the near future, certainly not Kit. Our relation with Hunthad is not very upbeat," the ruler said.

"In any case, he would surely tell us before leaving," said Ket.

"Kit has no business in that tower. It can only mean that he has been abducted and put in that tower by Hunthad's despotic ruler, Hunet. It occurs to me now that, the missing bodyguard was an immigrant from Hunthad. He might be a Hunthadian spy. We should have been more careful while recruiting him," inferred the ruler.

Dismayed, Ket sat down.

15

THE HUNTHADIANS

Hunthad, the vast tropical *yellow colour country* to the south of both Isthad and Inthad, is inhabited mostly by the yellow tailed Hunthadians. Millennia ago, a greatly gifted Hoo, by the name of Hun, had originated the *yellow colour* and unified the warring Hoo factions who lived in the lands where the daylight is predominantly yellow. Through his heavenly visions, Hun had realised the Supreme Unity in the form of the *yellow colour*. He was one of the pioneers who professed the unity of the entire Hoo race.

Interestingly, most of the Hoo wisdoms were broadly realised and revealed in the ancient times itself. Since then finer and finer details had been added to those broad sketches.

Now, Hun had realised this great wisdom that, *the highest level of existence of the Hoo race is possible only when the whole race has been united on a platform of equality*. But, due to the realities of the time in which he lived, his birth and upbringing in the tropical lands where the daylight is predominantly yellow and his own individual intuitive orientations and inclinations, he perceived that unity from his yellow perspective.

During Hun's time, those tropical lands were inhabited by mutually fighting savage tribes. His initial attempts to unify them by the light of his *wisdom of unity* yielded insignificant and unsustainable results. But, he was determined to manifest the wisdom into reality. Then it dawned upon him that the only way to effectively unify these savages was to take resort to force. He picked up the weapons and organised an army with his followers. The fire of his enlightenment sparked in his weapons. One by one, he subdued the tribes and transformed them into his *colour, yellow*, under the blessings of his *yellow deity, Huntha*. By the time Hun died, he had unified many of the tribes of the tropics and consolidated them into the huge *yellow colour country*, which he named *Hunthad.*

After Hun's death, there was none in Hunthad who was as resourceful as Hun himself. Gradually, the light of his wisdom faded away from the public memory. Only the exterior forms of his *yellow colour* remained giving the Hunthadians their unique *colour identity*. Literally following Hun's words and blindly emulating his actions, his scrupulous followers were caught within the ambit of Hun's *yellow colour*, which is, after all, only one of the innumerable possibilities of Hoo *colours*. Hun's followers wanted to paint the whole of the multi-coloured planet, Hoola, *yellow*. To achieve this, they even took recourse to militancy. War was in their ethos since times immemorial. For generations, the Hunthadians fought numerous battles and wars and transformed the conquered enemies into *yellow*. This went on for a thousand years. In the first few centuries, their war tactics proved pretty efficient and the *yellow colour* spread over large areas on Hoola. Then, these incessant wars gradually ebbed away their resources, their forces became fatigued and their militancy simply became unsustainable. Thus, they were compelled to come to a halt.

In the meantime, the Hunthadians' aggressive approach to unify the race through force and fear had made them unpopular among the other *colours*. Even now, there was an uneasy mistrust between the Hunthadians and the rest of the race.

16

HUNET

Hunthad is ruled from the *Yellow Palace* in the capital city of Gumba. This luxurious palace is built with a kind of locally available shining yellow stones and hence the name. It has all the amenities befitting monarchs: elaborate gardens with fountains, grand living quarters, banquet halls, elegant court rooms and more. At the centre of the palace is a huge round hall with circular galleries and balconies around an elevated podium.

On this day, as usual, the galleries were full with important Hoos from all over Hunthad. A trumpet was blown. The dignitaries present in the hall started chanting in unison, "Hunet, Hunet; Hunet, Hunet."

Amongst the cheers a finely crafted yellow metal throne gently ascended upon the podium from a hidden chamber below it. When the throne became completely visible, its occupant stood up and raised his rope like yellow tail. The chants gave way to complete silence. Hunet wore an intricately embellished yellow costume. He was of medium height, lean build and in his fifties. His slim and long face was crowned by porcupine-like straight hair. His beaky nose was flanked by his concave cheeks. He quickly looked around with his inquisitive and restless fox-like yellowish eyes.

After the ritualistic formalities, some day to day affairs of Hunthad were discussed and Hunet impressed his decisions on each and every one of those. Then, two over-sized Hunthadian soldiers dragged a prisoner into the circular hall through one of its many entrances and brought him before the throne. The prisoner could hardly stand on his feet. Still bleeding marks of slashes peeped out of his torn out brown apparel. One of the soldiers hailed, "Long live Hunet. We have administered the severe on this *sober* Sobret, just as you ordered."

"Hunet is pleased," said Hunet and ridiculed the prisoner. "Hope you liked the hospitality, you deplorable *sober*."

Insult added to his injury, the prisoner raised his anguished oval face and cried out, "Remember Hunet, my *sober* forefathers helped in building this palace, even the throne in which you are sitting. You can kill me but Lord Huntha will surely judge you one day."

Hunet continued to humiliate relentlessly, "I know what your forefathers did and that was all they could do, work. How dare the *sobers* misinterpret the books? They did not understand that words have meanings and there it all ends. They worked and they deserved to be ruled because none of them had the acumen to rule. Look at me. I am sitting in this throne because I am the one and only Hunet, the knowledgeable."

Before the prisoner could say anything else, the audience started chanting, "Hunet, Hunet; Hunet, Hunet."

Hunet gestured to the soldiers and the soldiers took the prisoner away. "I have an important appointment to keep," he said and abruptly stood up from his throne and raised his ropy tail. The trumpet blew again. The chanting continued. Hunet held his posture. Along with Hunet, the throne slowly descended and disappeared from the podium.

* * *

The mobile throne reached a lower chamber hidden below the level of the podium. Hunet stepped forward from the throne to meet his unwilling guest and said, "Welcome to Hunthad, Kit. Hope you enjoyed witnessing my rulings from here, on these live video display-screens."

Without responding to his suggestion Kit asked, "How did you bring me here?"

Hunet replied with a cunning smile, "My spies did a good job, just as I had asked them to. One of them, your trusted bodyguard, rendered you unconscious with an anesthetic Hunthadian herb and brought you out of your security zone. There, you were put into a high-altitude stealth flying car. Once the car rose to a height of ten kilometres above the Violet Land and resumed communication with the satellites, there was no problem in navigating back to Gumba. They nicely completed the operation in the cover of the night before anyone in Kithad noticed that you were missing.

"You focused a lot on your knowledge and economy. Wish you had taken more care for your security. I have this great talent of finding other's weaknesses, you see."

Kit defiantly asked, "Why have you brought me here?"

"Have patience, my friend. I have a lot of information about you; your achievements, your happy sweet family and your fame. How can you have all the good things that this world has to offer? What qualities do you possess that Hunet, the great, doesn't have?" remarked Hunet.

"Is that why you have abducted me; out of your utter envy at my well-being and happiness? If only you knew how much struggle and agony I had to go through to reach the present, all your envies would be extinguished," said Kit.

"O, I know how difficult this world is. I know very well that there is no free meal here. But you don't seem to know much about me. You have no idea how miserable life could be," said Hunet.

Kit maintained his calm and listened. Hunet continued, "We lived in a ghetto, a damp shanty in the northern part of Hunthad. My father was a labourer in the nearby *dine stone* mine. As you may know, the open-crust *dine* mines of Hunthad are scant in *dines*. Here the mining process is labour intensive and painstaking. My father toiled overtime in the heat of the *Let* to meet the two ends. Often he did miserably as the wages were very low. Sometimes, we even had to go hungry. At times my father took the frustration off his tired body and fatigued mind by finding faults with my mother and me on the most trivial of matters.

"My mother often wept silently; not because of how my father treated her but because she could not feed me enough. I understood my parents' helplessness and never complained. Even though lean and malnourished, since my childhood I had great memorising and cognitive powers. I could remember things simply by one read. But my parents could not afford to send me to school. I did not want to spend my life languishing like my father. I wanted to study and change my fate. I often visited the nearby town in search of books thrown away by the over-stuffed stupid children of my age who lived there. They went to schools and enjoyed their lives like hell simply because their parents had loads of money and elevated social status.

"I learnt, early in my life, that *money* and *power* are the two things people worship. Their tears of compassion have long dried up. True knowledge and piety have become things of the very distant past.

"Sometimes, my budding mind became furious at the yawning gap between their wastefulness and my utter poverty. I badly wanted to beat these scoundrels at their own game. I desperately looked for a glimmer of opportunity to change my fate and those of my poor parents. Luckily for me, that opportunity came by; sooner than I had expected.

"A charitable group visited our ghetto. They readily noticed my extraordinary gift. They picked me up and put me on a scholarship. For the first time in my life, I went to school. I added toil to my talents and broke one record after another. With the accolades, came respect. Now those fat scoundrels wanted to rub their shoulders against mine.

"But, before I could graduate, tragedy struck, not once but twice. One hot summer noon, my father succumbed to his prolonged hard labour. A few months later, incessant poverty took my mother away and brought an end to her ever degraded life. Even today, my heart anguishes like grave when I remember that I could not appease my parents.

"I kept my spirits up and focused on my studies. I learnt all the books of the Hunthadian tradition by heart.

By the time I graduated with unprecedented honours, I realised that no one in Hunthad was as knowledgeable as me. All I had to do since then was to use this knowledge to further my goal of raising the social echelons. It has not been a cake walk. I had to struggle hard to fend off steep competition posed by my competitors. But, in the end, no one could stand the power of my knowledge when I debated and spoke with the authority of the books.

"With power came money, unimaginable riches. Look at me. Today I am the number one Hoo in Hunthad, second only to Almighty, Huntha. I could not do anything for my parents while they were alive. But now, their souls must be happy that I have become the most powerful in Hunthad. But even this is not enough. Still there is more power to get. I want to rule all. I shall reach the top. Then all the Hoos will respect me and Hoola will be at my feet. I have to annex Kithad and take control of those *dine*-rich mines.

"But before that I shall have to come to terms with your international popularity. How can anyone else be more famous than me! I am the one and only, knowledgeable Hunet. Bad for you that you stand in my way. You have to go. When you are gone, so will be your fame. That is why you have been brought here. Don't be afraid. I shall be kind with you. You will be put to a deep, sound and peaceful sleep never to awake again," Hunet coldly said.

Kit kept his composure and, without blinking his eyes, said, "I have ever been submitted to the Supreme. The Supreme alone is the all-powerful ruler of this universe. All riches, all power and all knowledge belong to Him alone. We get to possess some of these only for a while. Then these are again reverted back to the Supreme.

"You can put an end to this body which I presently possess but my real existence is in my Soul, Divine. No sword can pierce It; fire cannot burn It; water cannot dissolve It. The Soul is finer than the fine and subtler than the subtle. If it is the Supreme's will that my Soul must leave my body here, then even you cannot prevent it. But, my Spirit will live on. The death of one Kit will surely give birth to thousands of Kits everywhere. How will you deal with them?"

"Go on. I am your patient listener," Hunet said cunningly.

"I am more worried about you, Hunet," Kit continued with serene sincerity. "Look, what you have done to yourself? Let's say, the entire Hoola comes under your feet. Will you be happy then? All your parents ever wanted was to see you smiling and happy. I see no smile on your face. I do not find any happiness in you."

Hunet's jaws toughened. Kit continued, "I am agonised to learn about the miseries of your childhood and the misfortune of your parents. But, you do not seem to realise that the strong impressions of these miserable experiences have kept your Soul ever tangled in the reactionary forces of *causes and effects*. Only your external realities have changed. Even now, are you not as miserable as you were at your childhood, my friend?"

Hunet remained silent. Kit paused and resumed, "In spite of learning all the Hunthadian books of wisdom by heart, your Soul is far from being liberated. This has happened because you have not been able to come to terms with your reactionary energies. Forgive, my friend; forgive your past, forgive your poverty, forgive your sufferings, forgive your misery and forgive your sorrow.

Only then, peace shall be yours. Liberation of the Soul can come only with the realisation that you are in all and all are in you; being happy at other's happiness and being sorry at other's misery. Have you done anything for the millions of Hunthadians who still live under the same conditions as those of your childhood? Even a fractional decrease in your offence and defence initiatives can alleviate their poverty."

"I was picked up for my extraordinary talents," interrupted Hunet. "How many are there who are as talented as me? None."

Kit replied, "Talented or not, every Hunthadian has a right to lead at least a decent life."

Now, Hunet's patience snapped. Agitatedly he said, "Who are you to preach me like that? You are not even a Hunthadian. I must rule because I am the best. Soldiers, take him back to the tower."

17

THOUGHT TRANSFERENCE

In the meantime, an anxious week passed since Kit went missing from Kithad. Then, one afternoon, Ket boarded the vertical car and went to the attic of the building of her apartment. This building raises two hundred storeys high into the sky. I, along with the kids, followed her. Let was halfway between the zenith and the horizon. She lit a sparkling star-like self-levitating blue light at a distance from us. As we watched, she took a fierce posture standing only on her right leg and aligned herself and her shivering tail towards the blue light. After a few minutes, the light started to move slowly. Ket turned to maintain her alignment towards the light. After turning a quarter of a circle, the light came to a standstill. Now, Ket faced south. The fierceness in her body language and the shivering of her tail gradually calmed down. Her eyes closed. She became immobile. My psychologist's eyes could read on her face that she had slipped into deep thought. *She must be lost in the thoughts of her beloved Kit,* I presumed.

* * *

Meanwhile, Hunet's spies brought him the news that the Kithadians had discovered that he had abducted Kit and put him at the top of the tower. His perfect abduction had been leaked. The spies also informed him that Kithadians leveraged on their good relations with most of the other *colour countries* to garner international pressure upon Hunthad to release Kit. Hunet's surreptitious ploy was to take on the other *colour countries* one by one and forcibly transform them into *yellow*. He knew, better than anyone else, that Hunthad would stand no chance against the rest of Hoola united. Overtly, he continued to deny the abduction.

On top of it, Hunet lost his patience with Kit. He could not stand the fact that even in captivity, Kit remained fearless and assertive. Most unbearably to him, all his bookish knowledge seemed miniscule before Kit's sheer wisdom and Kit made no effort to hide that. He saw the existence of Kit's personality as a mountainous obstacle between himself and his ambition to rule all of Hoola. He decided that Kit was better disposed of today than tomorrow. Enraged, Hunet changed his mind regarding putting Kit to a permanent sleep. Instead he directed his soldiers to throw him into the ancient *well of death* located about fifty kilometres south of the Hunthadian capital, Gumba.

The much dreaded *well of death* was constructed about four millennia ago a few centuries after the death of Hun, the Originator of the *yellow colour*. It was around this time that the fate of the *yellow colour* was at the crossroads. The Hunthadians were divided into two ideological factions. One side wanted to live the principle of Hun's universal brotherhood and bring an end to the war tactic. They professed that Hun had resorted to the war tactic as a temporary measure to unite the mutually fighting unruly tribes who lived on the equatorial lands during his time. The other side asserted that even though the *yellow colour country,* Hunthad, had come into existence, force was still necessary to discipline and transform all the Hoos into *yellow.* They were guided mainly by their submerged ancient warring ethos, which could not be appeased even by the great wisdoms of Hun, the great. In the ensuing struggle and civil war between the two factions, which lasted almost for half a century, eventually, the *sober* approach of the former faction gave way to the physical aggression of the latter.

The leaders of the former *sober* faction were captured by the leaders of the latter *extreme* faction who then became the *colour rulers* of Hunthad. These rulers wanted to serve the captives with exemplary punishment and raise a fear psychosis in the minds of the other Hunthadians with such *sober* tendencies. Thus they ordered the construction of the one kilometre deep well. After days of beastly torment and torture, the sober leaders were plunged into the well. Legends have it that, the shrill cries of their pain and agony were heard near the well for weeks. Then they died and their carcasses rotted in the murky water of the well. The whole atmosphere around the well became filthy and gloomy.

Four millennia had passed since then. Even now, Hoos of that area reported hearing the bone chilling cry of the unquenched souls of the condemned *sobers.*

Hunet would like to bring back the brutalities of the past but the international pressure on Hunthad to free Kit made him too impatient for the customary torture. He chose to immediately destroy the very evidence of the abduction, Kit himself. Kit was unceremoniously carried and plunged into the notorious *well of death.* As he hit the murky waters at the bottom of the well, the water splashed and something struck against the stone walls of the well. Were those the skeletal remains of the legendary condemned *sober* leaders? Kit could not figure out in the gloom. The air smelt damp and a bit pungent. He reckoned that the obnoxious microbes present in the place would decompose his body in a few days. Over his head, the mouth of the well seemed like a distant star, light-year away. On top of it, the creepiness of the haunted place soon started affecting his sensitive psyche. Then he heard the earnest call of the condemned *sobers*, as loud as his own voice, "Why have you come here? Have you forgotten that you have works to do for the race? Go away from here, Kit."

Faced with imminent death, Kit desperately prayed, "O Lord, if it is your will that my soul should leave my body like this, then so be it. But, O, the kindest One, for one more time, let me hold the tranquility of my son, Sook, and the delight of my daughter, Soor, in my arms. For one more time, let me behold the radiant blue eyes of my beloved Ket and let me caress her face."

Then, out of the darkness in his psyche, arose a beautiful voice, the voice that he wanted to hear the most, saying, "Why dost thou despair, my love? Despair not. Thou art not alone even for a moment. Me is always with thee."

"O dearest Ket!" exclaimed Kit. "My heart remains ever with thee and shall unceasingly be thine."

Then he heard her singing the soulful song,

"Thou art in me
And me is in Thee.

Because of Thee,
I be."

All of Kit's agonies vanished immediately. Ket solemnly affirmed, "This cannot be the end. We cannot lose each other yet again. I shall not let that happen. Remember, we have the blessings of the Lord's love. Our love must triumph over the hatred and hostilities of this world. Neither you nor I fear the separatist hatred."

"But, how will I be able to come out of this well?" asked Kit.

"Why not?" promptly assured Ket. "Have you forgotten that at one stage during your enlightenment through alignment, you attained the power to levitate? You had forgone that power then, in search of yet higher enlightenment. That power is still within you. Recall that power now and multiply it. You will surely raise yourself out of this well."

"O dear, you have just raised my hopes of seeing Sook and Soor again. Where would I be without you!" said Kit. He sang,

"Because of Thee-
I be.

At every single moment,
Thou makest me."

After the emotions settled down, Kit informed Ket, "Dear Ket, there is another serious issue at hand. Hunet is planning to conquer the other *colour countries*, one at a time, and transform all into *yellow*. He wants to rule all of Hoola. Kithad is his first target. His spies are everywhere. His heartless cruelty never stops hurting others. If he succeeds, it will only mean misery, plunder and massacre.

"Hunet must be stopped before he becomes too powerful. Tell everyone to prepare for the imminent war."

* * *

After almost ten impatient minutes, Ket slowly opened her eyes. She looked disturbed.

I softly asked, "What happened?"

Holding back her tears, she replied in an anguished voice, "Hunet has thrown him into the *well of death.* They say that no one has ever come out alive from that dreaded well." She paused as the rest of us were dumbstruck. Then the kids hurried to their mother. She hugged them. Then she looked skywards and cried, "Lord Intha, how can you let this happen. He is submitted to do your work. If our love is pure then send him back to me."

The kids were weepy too. Trying to placate them, I asked Ket, "How can you be so sure? There may be a mistake."

Ket gently turned to me and said, "I just spoke to him. Right now he is in that well."

A combined feeling of astonishment and agony filled me now. On Earth, I had read many western and eastern references to *thought transference* and *telepathy* and their numerous possibilities. But this was the first time I witnessed such a thing happening before my very eyes.

Is it because, their elevated psyches are so much in tune with each other in an amazing rapport that they are able to instantaneously exchange their thoughts over long distances without any conductor or medium? Or is it because of the evolutionary development of these aliens. I could not figure out. Anyway, this was not the time to indulge in these thoughts. I told Ket, "Let us go downstairs. We have to act fast."

18

WAR

Ever since Hunet had risen to the helm of affairs of Hunthad, there had been international concerns about his secret designs. He centralised the ruling powers of Hunthad and vested all the important charges, including defence, security, finance, justice and internal affairs, unto himself. Only a few charges like civic amenities, health and education were left to his heavily subordinated ministers. These ministers led a life of opulence but often they failed in alleviating the miseries of the common Hunthadians. Because even though the taxes were high, most of the Hunthadian resources were sucked up in acquisition of weapons, recruitment of soldiers and maintenance of the over-sized Hunthadian military. Suitable and young Hunthadians from the poorer sections of the society were either enticed or forced to join the military; farmers, labourers and miners, none were spared. The soldiers led a better life than the common Hunthadians who were compelled to toil and thus exploited for the resources.

By now, the Hunthadian army had grown to a size of more than four times larger than what was required to defend Hunthad effectively.

The information, passed on by Kit to Ket through *thought transference,* about Hunet's surreptitious motives to annex the other *colour countries* and establish his absolute rule all over Hoola reached every corner of the planet overnight and shocked the global peoples. It vindicated the growing suspicion on Hunet among the other *colour countries.*

Hunthad meets the southern ocean at its eastern shores. The *green* and the *orange colour countries* respectively to the west and south of Hunthad cordoned and sealed their borders with the *yellow colour country.* To the north of Hunthad are Isthad and Inthad. These two neighboring *colour countries* had traditionally been at war with each other. Kit had been able to narrow the gap between these two and had revealed the common parentage of the Originators of their respective *colours.* Now, for the first time, the Inthadian and Isthadian forces joined hands with the Kithadian army against a common enemy. Hunet had planned to wedge his soldiers through the border between Isthad and Inthad and reach Kithad. But, now he was faced with the attack by the formidable combined forces of these three *colour countries.* The trio wanted to not only rescue Kit but also protect themselves and other *colour countries* from the Hunthadian aggression under Hunet and his voracious designs.

Most of the other *colour countries* went into the war alert. Thus, after five hundred years of the third global war, which had almost turned Hoola into dust, the planet was about to witness the similar kind of bloodbath and destruction. All weapons of mass destruction and firearms were prohibited and dismantled on Hoola by an international convention subsequent to the third global war. Machines and cars were also not allowed in the battle. But, even the metal and other weapons that were presently in use on technologically advanced Hoola were more alien than the wildest imagination and had tremendous destructive powers.

The combined forces closed in on Hunthad from the north. They enjoyed the moral and logistics support from many other medium and small sized *colour countries*. With only a shoreline at its eastern border, the mostly landlocked Hunthad was under serious trade embargo. They were compelled to depend solely on their internal resources. Nevertheless, the Hunthadian military was no less formidable. Hunthad is a vast tropical landmass with bountiful resources. The Hunthadians had a long history of warrior-ship since the ancient times. Battle was in their blood. The sheer size of the *yellow* forces with many years of preparations was awesome. These fierce fighters were stirred by Hunet in the name of their *yellow-ship*. Most importantly, they were on their home territory and acclimatised with the tropics.

As expected, they put up steep resistance to the advance of the combined forces.

19

SOBRET

In the meantime, a little while after Kit's *thought transference* with Ket, a heavy object splashed into the water of the *well of death.* Kit stretched his hands and tail to grope in the darkness. It was another Hoo. Kit quickly pulled it up from the bottom and held its head above the murky water. It was in a bad shape and had little consciousness left in it. Kit asked, "Who are you?"

The Hoo could hardly speak but before passing out completely struggled to whisper, "Sobret."

Kit remembered that this was the tortured *sober* Hunthadian whom he had seen in the circular hall of the Yellow Palace at Hunet's assembly. *If I be able to raise myself out of this well, I shall take him along with me.* He resolved in his mind.

The Hoos had mastered the antigravity technology using highly sophisticated machines and magnetism. But the levitation, that Kit had been reminded of by Ket, was a positive byproduct of his spiritual upliftment through alignment, a mastery of his mind over his body.

He held Sobret against his body by coiling his tail around. Then he bifurcated his mind; while one part remained aware of his environment, the other part dived inwards and merged into deep alignment. His being became calm and poised. Now he controlled his nerve-currents using his life-breath. Gradually, his inner light grew brighter and brighter in his consciousness. His psychic forces became perfectly balanced through all the extreme points of his body, the tips of his fingers, toes, tail and the crown of his head. Thus, he recalled his forgotten power to make his body lighter than the air and levitated a few feet above the water in the well. Thereafter, as prompted by Ket, he multiplied this process and within a couple of hours raised himself to the mouth of the one kilometre deep well, along with Sobret. Then he retreated from the alignment and the two halves of his mind converged.

Kit gently laid Sobret on the ground, wiped the water off his body with his furry tail and brought him back to his senses. Sobret said to him, "Thank you for saving my life. From now on, I shall remain ever grateful to you. But, who are you? I have never seen anyone with such a white tail."

"I am Kit from Kithad," replied Kit.

Hearing this, Sobret, in spite of his wounds, became excited and said, "O, I have heard about you and your fantastic feats. It's incredible that now I meet you in person. I should have guessed. Who else could have come out alive from this well!"

Then he aligned himself to Kit. Kit reciprocated Sobret's alignment and said, "You would have done the same thing if you were in my place. Relax Sobret. Control your excitement. You need rest. I shall take care of you until you fully recover."

"Let's get away from this place, my savior," said Sobret.

"But, where should we go? Hunet's spies must be everywhere," asked Kit.

"That is true. But, in spite of the fear of Hunet's persecutions, the *sobers* have remained pandemic, scattered in small groups. Even though marginalised from the main stream of the Hunthadian society, we have preserved the legacy of our forefathers and maintained our moderate approach to the wisdom of Hun. By the divine grace of Almighty Huntha, we have endured the predicaments over thousands of years," said Sobret.

"Your endurance will soon bear its deserved fruits," affirmed Kit.

Sobret continued, "I know a place twenty kilometres north of here at the edge of the tropical forests where such a group of *sobers* live and practice the *sober* hue of the *yellow colour*. But I am not sure if I can make it to that village in my present condition."

Kit reassuringly said, "Don't worry. I shall carry you there. You just show me the way."

Then he picked up Sobret's battered physique on his back. Thereafter, Kit walked nonstop. Sobret guided him through the relatively secluded places in the cover of the night while most of Hunthad rested.

They reached the small village in the morning. The farmers were leaving their homes for the day's work in the fields. In spite of the developments elsewhere in Hunthad, these marginalised *sobers* carried simplistic and old equipments with them. Surprised and shocked, they received the duo and took them in. With the help of the villagers, Kit devoted himself to taking care of Sobret. In degrees, Sobret recovered over several days.

* * *

During these days, Hunthad had been attacked by the combined forces from the north. The fearless Hunthadian forces put up steep resistance. Arrows rained, spears cleaved, catapults threw up heavy boulders kilometres ahead on the uneven terrains of the battlefield in the searing heat of the tropical summer. The first couple of days went like this with neither side giving an inch. By the third day, the combined forces had gauged the Hunthadian military. The combined forces had a slight advantage with the longer range of their catapults. To make the most of this advantage, they advanced their most efficient artillery division while maintaining enough distance so that the Hunthadian ballistics could not reach them. But their longer range artillery landed well into the Hunthadian lines giving the combined forces their first vital opening.

As already mentioned, about five centuries earlier, the third global war on Hoola had almost destroyed the planet. Subsequently, to save the planet from annihilation, all sorts of firearms, air and automated attacks had been prohibited on Hoola by a convention of all the *colour countries*. Thereafter, the infantry had become the most important in Hoo warfare.

Now, the infantry of the combined forces were able to move forward southwards under the protective ballistics of their longer range catapults. Thus, yard by yard, the Hunthadian forces were forced to recede.

20

THE TUNNEL

One day the news reached the *sobers'* village that, the combined forces had reached the outskirts of Gumba, the capital of Hunthad. Hunet's enemies were at his threshold. At this point, it was presumed that Hunet's days were counted and the war would soon reach its conclusion. But, ten more days of intense fighting passed and still the combined forces could not enter Gumba. All the projectiles from their arsenals were mysteriously repelled back by the city and it stubbornly fended off all their attacks. Virtually, it seemed more like a prolonged stalemate.

By this day, Sobret's wounds had almost healed. But the wounds that had been inflicted in his mind stayed anguishing fresh. After hearing about the stalemate, he confided to Kit, "Ten days are nothing. Gumba can hold on to this siege for ten years or even more. By then, Hunet will surely find his way to shock the world. Gumba is a self-sustaining city. It runs on the principle of recycling of the resources. Hunet's talents go beyond his knowledge of the Book Reverend. His ruthless tactics and war strategies are shrewd and effective. For many years, he has been planning and preparing to take Hoola and he is ready to face all possible eventualities. Now, he must have activated the energy shield to cover Gumba."

"Energy shield!" exclaimed Kit.

"Yes. The shield is so powerful that even the banned weapons of mass destruction would not be able to breach it. The spears and arrows of the combined forces do not even feel like wire-pins to the shield. They are simply wasting their energies and resources. Gumba is practically impregnable," said Sobret.

"But, such an energy shield must have cost a heaven to create and Hunthad is hungry," opined Kit.

"Yes. More than half of the total domestic produce of Hunthad is collected as taxes. A lion-share of those taxes goes into the defence expenditure while many Hunthadians suffer from poverty and die of starvation," said Sobret.

"Is there absolutely no way?" asked Kit.

Sobret thought for several minutes. Then he said, "There may be a remote chance of getting to Hunet. There is a highly guarded secret about the Yellow Palace, which has been passed on to me through generations of my ancestors.

"The palace was first built three and a half thousand years ago. This was the time when Hunthad witnessed frequent battles and volatility. During the next two and a half thousand years, Hunthad came under the rule of one despot after another. The coveted throne of Hunthad was an insecure place to be. During these two and a half millennia, the Yellow Palace was completely destroyed and rebuilt as many as five times.

"The construction of the present palace was started a thousand years ago. The *sober* architects of that time were employed for the construction work for their skillfulness.

The chief architect was my distant ancestor. It took many years to complete the first palace. It was a wonder of that time. To ensure that such a wonder is not replicated, the contemporary despotic ruler of Hunthad ordered the slaughter of the chief architect. But, before the order could be carried out, my forefather and a few of his mates managed to escape from the slavery through a secret way.

"Since then, that secret has been passed on through generations and presently only I know that secret. There may be a suspicion about me in Hunet. Perhaps that is why he wanted to kill me. However, I do not know how relevant that secret may be in the present time. In the last one thousand years, the palace has undergone many renovations, alterations, expansions and modernisations and has become what it is today."

"Forget about the odds. Tell me the secret. Let's give it a try. Because there is no other way," said Kit.

Sobret said, "At some point of time during the construction of the first phase of the present palace, my forefather had sniffed the dismal fate that the ruler would mete out to him after the completion of the work. So he told a few of his close mates to secretly dig a tunnel through the basement of the under-construction palace. The tunnel had to be long enough to take them away from the city of Gumba. For years, they dug the underground tunnel while the palace and the city grew on the ground.

"On the day of the escape, they entered the tunnel and sealed the opening of the tunnel behind them. The other end of the tunnel is several kilometres away from here, at the Yellow Hills in the dense recesses of the dreaded Yellow Forest."

Kit inferred, "So, we can reach the basement of the Yellow Palace through that tunnel and bypass the energy shield, which is above the ground."

"Right. But first we have to cover the dense forest to reach the mouth of the tunnel. Besides, in the last thousand years many changes have taken place. There have been earthquakes and landslides. The present condition of the nineteen kilometre long tunnel is unknown," said Sobret.

"If this is our only chance then let's not waste our time. Each day, innocent soldiers are dying due to one Hoo's insatiable greed. Hunet must be stopped at the earliest," said Kit.

Thus, they invited volunteers from among the *sober* villagers. The *sobers* saw this as an unprecedented opportunity to not only alleviate their degraded position in the Hunthadian society under Hunet but free Hunthad itself from the tyrannical clutches of Hunet. They decided that it is better to die like a hero than live every day in utter deprivation and agreed to go on the secret operation under Kit's leadership.

Kit picked up a handful of young and able males. Though they were not soldiers, some of them were good tillers; some others were good at using the axe to chop off big trees and so on. They picked up whatever equipment and weapons that they found handy. Kit was provided with the weapon of his choice, a sword.

The dense tropical Yellow Forest is full of huge, centuries old Yellow trees with their canopies rising to a hundred metres high and permanently shading the soils below. These alien trees never shed their leaves, which are more yellow than green and hence the name. Several other species of parasites and creepers grow on these Yellow trees.

The daylight of *Let* hardly ever reaches the ground below. The ground is covered with dense vegetation of numerous strange looking smaller plants and shrubs some of which bear peculiar flowers and precarious fruits. The soil of the Yellow Forest is damp and carpeted by fallen leaves, twigs and other plant parts.

The forest provides a rich habitat to innumerable alien insects, birds and animals. But the dread of the Yellow Forest comes mainly from a particular animal, the *pangor*. This ferocious six legged top of the food-chain agile carnivore with ten inch long fangs knows no competition and rules the Yellow Forest, both on the ground as well as among the canopies. This six legged stealth predator can climb the trees. At times, the animals visit the villages in the periphery of the forest and take domestic animals though they rarely attack a Hoo. The *sobers'* village is one such village.

Now, the ingenuous team that Kit had selected from among the villagers entered the shadowy Yellow Forest. They were guided by Sobret who knew the way to the opening of the secret tunnel to the Yellow Palace. Their leader, Kit was the only true warrior in the team. The moist air in the forest smelt fragrant with the scent of exotic herbs. They heard only the chirping of small insects, occasional calling of exotic birds and bone-chilling howling of wild animals. A wild *pangor* could attack from any direction, left, right, front, back and above.

It was not easy to move through that dense vegetation. They had to chop off plants and branches to make their way. After covering some distance, Kit said to everyone, "Be alert, I have this creepy feeling that we are being followed."

A kilometre hence, Kit's intuition horribly turned true. Their pursuer had been moving silently behind them. Its yellow fur with brownish patches perfectly camouflaged it among the branches of the Yellow trees. Before they knew it, the king of the Yellow Forest greeted them with its ten inch long dagger like fangs pierced into the left thigh of Jik, the tiller, who had fallen back forty metres behind the rest. It was a fully grown male *pangor,* twenty feet long from the head to tail and at least a thousand pound in weight. Robust, two hundred and fifty pound Jik coiled his tail around the *pangor's* neck to stop its breath, hit its head with his tilling equipment and tried his best to free himself from the hungry beast. But his resistances were too feeble to the animal. In no time, it fixed Jik to the ground with its forepaws and mid-legs and sunk two of its fangs in Jik's head. Then the animal leaped off with Jik's body in its grasp and disappeared among the branches of the Yellow trees before anyone could reach out to Jik. The Yellow Forest had claimed its first casualty.

As tragic and as horrific as the mishap was, there was little time to mourn Jik's death. The animal knows neither good nor evil. It kills out of its instinct to satisfy its hunger. But the Hoo, whom they sought, put the lives of tens of millions of innocent Hunthadians in endless misery and jeopardy for his utter conceit and insatiable greed.

Grieved, they quietly moved on. Then, the general quiet of the forest was perturbed by a faint but continuous sound of falling water coming from a distance. Sorbet said, "We are almost there. Let's follow that sound."

Gradually, the faint sound turned into a roar. It was clear that they were approaching a gigantic waterfall.

After another half a kilometre, they heard the noise of the waterfall loud and clear and they knew that they were very near to it. Still the waterfall was hidden from their vision. That is why they called it the Hidden Waterfall. After trekking a few hundred metres more, they reached the foot of the Yellow Hills. Then they went over the first ridge of the hills through its dense vegetation and the mighty and magnificent waterfall revealed itself. Sorbet said, "The mouth of the tunnel should be somewhere here."

They scanned every square metre of that area but could not find the tunnel. Was the secret of the tunnel a truth or had they been running after a figment losing the life of Jik in the process. Sorbet was tense but he reaffirmed, "The tunnel must be here. My scrupulous forefathers would not make such a joke."

Kit told him, "Look Sobret, there is only one place left to be rummaged and that is behind that column of the falling water."

He asked one of the villagers to use his sling and hurl a stone right through the falling water. Just as Kit had guessed, the stone went right through the water column and after a couple of seconds came the reverberating sound of the stone hitting some hollow place on the other side. "Oh, the tunnel is there! But how to reach it?" said Sobret.

Kit pointed to a hundred feet tall straight trunk Yellow tree and said, "If we can chop off that trunk and put it in place through the side of the falling waters where the flow is less severe, then we have a chance."

As Kit said, so they did. Felling the tree was like bread and butter for the axe-men. Soon the job was completed.

Then Kit asked them to stand in a line behind him facing the waterfall. Each held the tail of the Hoo standing before him. This increased stability and ensured that if anyone slipped while walking on the log, the others could rescue him.

Thus, they reached the mouth of the nineteen kilometre long tunnel. They switched on their torches and ventured into the claustrophobic, uncertain darkness of the tunnel. Anything could happen there. There could be dangerous animals burrowing in the tunnel. Then, there could be some obnoxious poisonous gas accumulated in it over the centuries. Even a mild earthquake could bury all of them alive and they would never see the light of day again. But, in their minds they had already overcome death.

Fortunately for them and amazingly, but for a few blockages, the tunnel had withstood well the test of a thousand years'. The tillers did good work at digging the way through the bottlenecks and blockages. At times, the end of the tunnel seemed near and yet it was so far. The tunnel seemed unending. Their progress was slow and laborious. But, they persevered and, at last, reached the other end of the tunnel. But there was no light at the end of that tunnel. Before them was a large block of yellow stone cube, the stone with which the Yellow Palace had been constructed.

21

IN THE YELLOW PALACE

They did not know what awaited them at the other side of the block of stone. So, they carefully chipped the block and made a hole through it. They found a small vacant stone compartment.

One by one, they came out of the tunnel into the congestion of the stone compartment, which seemed like a vacant space in the basement. Once out of the tunnel, Kit, the warrior, came to his being. There was a small trapdoor at a corner of the room. In no time, Kit opened the trapdoor using his sword. Then they entered a passage. Hunet's guards could be there around every corner. They cautiously proceeded through the passage. The air was a bit stinky. Then they heard the first sound in the palace other than their own breathing and whispers. It was an intermittent sound of groaning in pain. As they followed the sound, the stink of the air became prominent. The groan was coming from around the corner ahead of them. Kit peeped around the corner to find a horrible sight.

There was a large open space of the basement with several stone pillars in it. Metal chains and rings were fastened to each pillar. Skinny prisoners were tied to some of the pillars. They looked starved and tortured. While a few groaned intermittently, others appeared to be unconscious. Or were they dead already? Kit slowly entered the room. The prisoner chained to the nearest pillar noticed him and taking him for a palace guard, cried out, "Don't hurt me anymore. I cannot stand the pain of my wounds. I don't remember when I ate or drank the last time. You better kill me now."

Kit gestured at him to be silent, went near him and whispered in his ears, "Don't be afraid, friend. We have come to rescue you."

They gave water and some food to the prisoners and set them free from the shackles and fetters. The brief conversations revealed that some of these prisoners were either *sobers* whom Hunet abhorred the most or youths who had refused to join the military. The rest were charged with various offences. The prisoners also said that there were others put behind the bars in the cells adjacent to this area of the basement, awaiting the fate of these prisoners.

Thus, the basement bore the signatures of Hunet's tyranny. Perhaps, in the urgency to defend the palace, the guards were mostly deployed at its gates and periphery. An intrusion through the basement was not expected and so the basement was left relatively unguarded. Kit asked his squad to free all the prisoners and wait in the basement for his signal. He, Sobret and two others took the stairs to the upper floor. The door at the end of the stair was ajar. Two soldiers guarded the door from the outside. Kit and his people burst open the door and took them by surprise. Before the soldiers could react both of them were down. Then they passed through a corridor and came before a door with delicate designs curved on it. Above the door was written a word in Hoo language which means 'treasury'. This door was towards the internal side of the palace. It was locked from inside and there were no soldiers guarding it. Kit and his people broke open the door. The treasury was a huge room with safes, vaults and chests. They opened one chest. It was full of jewels, ornaments and precious stones. Kit said to Sobret, "This treasury can make our world rich but poor Hunthadians are starving. We will come back to this place later. Let's now find Hunet."

They went across the treasury to its main entrance door, which was closed from the outside. It was obvious that there would be guards outside the treasury. So they positioned themselves on either side of the door, ready with their weapons. Then Kit made a hard knock on the door with the handle of his sword. As expected, soon the door opened and half a dozen soldiers entered the room. Before they could raise an alarm, Kit and his fellows attacked them from behind and got the better of them. They tied and gagged five of the soldiers. Kit placed the tip of his sword at the sixth, relatively frail, soldier's throat and sternly asked him, "Where is Hunet?"

Shaking with fear, the soldier replied, "He is in the central hall with his generals."

"Take us to the hidden chamber below the podium of the central hall. If you make any false move I shall cut you to pieces," ordered Kit.

Thus they were taken to the hidden chamber. They locked the exit door from inside, tied and gagged the frail soldier and hid him behind a stone column. On the video display of the hidden chamber they saw Hunet sitting in his throne. His generals and officers sat in the gallery. Hunet was as animated as ever. He said, "Brave soldiers of Hunthad, we must bring the prophecy of the Book Reverend to reality at any cost. The thirteenth chapter of the Book clearly mentions that all Hoos should live in unity. Lord Huntha shall be pleased with us and bless us with His riches when we achieve this. I know how to handle the present attack on Hunthad. We will teach them a good lesson. Prepare the fusion bomb."

"But Hunet, what about the international ban on the use of weapons of mass destruction? Millions of civilians will be killed and generations will be crippled if we use the nuke. Moreover, it could snowball into a global war and destroy Hoola itself," opined one of his generals.

"Ah! Nothing is above the Book Reverend, you fool. With the fusion bomb we will unite the race into our *yellow colour*. This is an extreme situation. So, extreme measures are necessary. Our *colour* is in danger. It doesn't matter whether Hoola remains or goes. Our *yellow colour* must live on," pronounced Hunet.

No one dared to ask Hunet *where the yellow colour would be if Hoola itself was gone?* Someone from the gallery shouted, "Long live, the *yellow colour*."

Then, everyone repeated in chorus, "Long live, the *yellow colour*."

Hunet arose from his throne and ordered, "Prepare the fusion bomb."

Everyone chanted, "Hunet, Hunet; Hunet, Hunet."

The trumpet blew. Hunet held his posture. The throne descended and disappeared from the podium.

As usual, the mobile throne came to the hidden chamber below the podium where Kit and his mates were hiding to greet Hunet. Hunet stepped into the chamber. His face looked stern with authority and his ropy tail was still hoisted upwards. Then, it was the moment of truth for him. Suddenly, he was surrounded by Kit, Sobret and the other two *sobers*. Before Hunet could react, the tip of Kit's sword was at the despot's throat. They quickly tied him to the throne. Shocked beyond his wits to see both Kit and Sobret alive, Hunet's tail dropped and so did his jaw. His nervous yellowish eyes grew as restless as ever. Kit calmly but firmly said, "Any false move and your chance to a fair trial will end here and now."

Getting over the effects of his first shock, Hunet tried to muster some courage and said, "I don't know how you got here but there is no way you will get away alive from here. Drop your arms and I may be lenient to you."

"I have had enough taste of your leniency, Hunet. You have done all the harm that you can do. Your time is over now. By the name of Lord Huntha and for the sake of the innocent Hunthadians, I seize your ruling powers and arrest you," said Sobret.

Hunet found that his first tact to raise fear in their hearts failed. Faced with imminent disaster, he resorted to his time-tested weapon, the best weapon he had ever known, his ability to debate. Amazingly, in his mind even now he seemed sure that he could not only justify all his past actions but also win over his adversaries with his words. He said, "I am Hunet, the wise. No one knows the *Book Reverend of Hunthad* better than I do. I rule Hunthad by the authority of the Book. Everything I have ever done was for the sake of our *Yellow colour*. I worked my heart out to manifest the prophecy of unity of the Hoos as stated in the Book."

Now, Kit said, "Books can be a Hoo's good friend. There are books full of knowledge on every conceivable subject: science, economics, history, arts, literature, philosophy and so on. Then, there are books written by outstanding authors who have mastered the art of writing interesting and entertaining stories. There is also another genre of books whose scripts purport and deliver great inspiring wisdom.

"The third kind of books has had the most profound and long lasting effects on the psyche of our race. While some of these effects have been immensely beneficial to the Hoos, the others have been equally harmful. Most devastatingly, the exclusive reliance on any one of these *colour scriptures* has caused the fragmentation of every aspect of the existence of our race; from the internal psychological space to the outward physical space giving rise to, among other evils, *inter colour conflicts*.

"Today, there is a need for a new book written with earnest and brave aspiration, envisaging an attempt at bridging the enormous gulfs of *colour differences* that have been caused by the exclusive reliance on any one of the existing *colour scriptures*."

Hunet interrupted, "But, aren't *equality* and *unity* great ideals?"

Kit explained, "*Equality* and *unity* may be extreme ideals but *freedom* and *harmony* are a more pragmatic approach to come to terms with the reality of the *diversity* that is existent in the Hoo race. For *freedom* and *harmony, diversity* must be accommodated.

"But, in their obsession with *equality, the extreme Hunthadians* forgot the *diversity* of nature. Ages of psychological grooming effected by their traditional conditioning made them want to paint the whole of multi-coloured Hoola with their monochromatic *yellow*. And you, Hunet, took full advantage of this psychological grooming of your compatriots to advance your selfish designs mainly by misinterpreting the Hunthadian *Book Reverend.* Originator of the *yellow colour*, Hun, and the subsequently written *Book Reverend* profess the unity of the race but neither dictates the destruction of freedom of all under a dictator.

"Why should everyone be called Hunet? Why should we have to paint our planet with a monochrome *yellow*? The moment you give a *name* and a *form*, you inevitably limit the infinite potency inherent in the innumerable diversity existent in the Hoo race. Seven billions of us are here on Hoola; so similar and yet, each one of us is so unique with unique physique, personality, intellect, temperament, needs, desires, hopes, aspirations and so on. Then, how can there be a single *panacea* which may suit all?

"Through different series of '*causes and effects*' we, the Hoo race, have come this far where we find ourselves segregated into 300 odd *colour countries*, which, in turn, have segregated our psychological internal space as well. Interestingly, our basic and prime goals remain the same: to reach the truth and to come to terms with our existence, as it is, and to realise the essence behind that existence both externally as well as internally.

"Every child is born pure, pristine and free. It descends from freedom and then it gradually imbibes all these contaminations from its external environments, which are anything but perfect. We, grown-ups, have already been contaminated enough to merely reflect the externality in which we find ourselves. As we have dived into ignorance, our visions have become narrow and blurred and we are unable to see the truth. No matter how we may like to distinguish ourselves, after all, we are one Hoo race, the multitude of external manifestations of that one Supreme Being, one Spirit and one Soul from Whom we have descended.

"While it may be important to preserve, maintain and develop the unique identity of each *colour entity*, it is more vital to simultaneously remain aware of the entire *whole* of which each is a part and parcel.

"The name *Book Reverend* implies that it is not an inert object, not a mere collection of words with only meanings attached to those. It is a personality and Its essence is in Its *spirit*.

"Hunet, you have mugged up the *Book Reverend* word by word, learnt the meanings of those words and stopped there. You never made the effort to realise the *Book's spirit* and live that realisation from inside out. You have not witnessed any ascent in your own *spirit*. Your *spirit* has remained where it was before you read the *Book Reverend*. This is why, even now, you selfishly want to control all and transform everyone into *yellow* without giving any heed to the others' freedom and their inherent right to choice of *colour*.

"See, where you stand now. In your plight to rob others of their freedom, you have lost your own. Your intolerance of others was bound to, sooner or later, evoke intolerance for you in the others.

"Unity by force has an inherent disadvantage. As soon as the force is taken away, that unity falls apart. Because each Hoo aspires for the freedom to be the way it is. Life under duress is agonising and unfulfilling. *Unity can come from Love alone, by expanding the Self to transcend all barriers and encompass all, as they are.*"

For the first time, Hunet's most effective weapon, his power to debate, did not work. All his reasoning efforts convinced none and fell apart before the pure and unselfish wisdom of Kit. Fear started to grip his being now. He tried to hide his fear and said, "Kit, I understand now that you are the best and not me. I shall make all the arrangements to return you to Kithad with full state honour. Forgive me."

Kit smiled and serenely said, "That won't be necessary. I shall return to Kithad anyway. I forgive you but there are millions of others to whom you owe countless apologies.

"Now, tell your soldiers that you have transferred all your ruling powers to Sobret. Our *sober* friends are waiting at the prison. Ask your guards to free all the illegally arrested political prisoners. Hand over the charges of the Yellow Palace to the *sober* villagers and make all the arrangements so that we can reach the *tower*."

22

TOWARDS PEACE

Thus, Hunet was allowed to speak to his soldiers with his wrist gadget. Then all of them boarded the throne. The mobile throne rose upon the podium of the circular hall. This time, there was no trumpet, no chanting. The hall was vacant. Kit said to Hunet, "Now let us go straight to the tower."

Thereafter, Sobret, the new ruler of Hunthad, and his two *sober* guards took Hunet and escorted Kit atop the famous *tower of Gumba.* Sobret said through the public announcement system, "I, the ruler of Hunthad, declare an immediate and unilateral cease-fire and call upon the combined forces for an armistice under the auspices of none other than the great Kit, the ruler of Kithad, who is presently our guest of honour."

Kit asserted, "Hunet has been arrested. I urge the Kithadian and combined forces to end this bloodshed immediately. Sobret will remain in the throne until complete peace returns to Hunthad. Then the Hunthadians will decide their own future free from the despotic tyranny of Hunet. Hunet's fate will be decided by the Hunthadians themselves.

"Here is a little food for thought to avert such a situation from recurring. *It may be inherently hazardous to exclusively cling on to a single colour; for, in doing so, the others who are not part of that colour tradition are excluded; thus, augmenting to that eternal divisive force, which has been the root cause of most of the miseries throughout the Hoo history.*

"The 'Whole' is the Lord. In each, I perceive myself and in me, I find every other. I find myself in a continuous fluid of the Hoo race.

"Who is meant to serve for whom, the colours for the Hoos or the Hoos for the colours?

"Closing the door and shutting the windows to each other's respective realities will only widen the gulf of differences. Let us foster greater understanding about the Hunthadians and their *yellow colour* among the other *colours* and about the others and their *colours* among the Hunthadians to bring home the positives in each side and try to bridge the widening gap between the two, the single largest source of division of the race.

"I wish Hunthad peace and prosperity."

The news of the announcements was soon broadcast all over Hoola.

Thus, the armistice was effected but not without severe constraints on Hunthad. The protective energy shield over Gumba was partially switched off to let an elite brigade of the combined forces enter the picturesque architectural city and take control of its important installations. This brigade maintained piece and ensured that anarchy did not set in after Hunet's fall. These peacekeepers did not enter the Yellow Palace, which was now controlled by the *sober* Hunthadians. Hunet's secret weapons of mass destruction, the fusion bombs, were dismantled.

Sobret gave the following undertakings on behalf of Hunthad. Henceforth, the Hunthadians would give up the policy of forceful transformation of the other *colours* into their *yellow* and foster among themselves respect for the other *colours* just as they respect their own *yellow colour*. They would never attack or harm any other *colour country*. The Hunthadian army and its armament would be cut to a size enough for its own defence. No Hunthadian would be forced to join the Hunthadian army against its will.

Hunet's treasury was opened and his fortune was used for the welfare of the poor Hunthadians. Hunet was tried for torture, exploitation and murder of innocent Hunthadians and for dragging Hunthad to the war and degrading Hunthad before the global community. He was sentenced to be thrown into the *well of death*. The spirits of the ancient condemned *sobers* suffocated him in the murky waters of the well and set his soul free from the clutches of his own greed, conceit and devilish selfishness.

All the while Kit remained in Gumba and organised the peacekeeping efforts of the combined forces. He also advised Sobret on the ways to usher in peace and prosperity to Hunthad. Kit's family, I and few of his Kithadian administrators were flown into Gumba. Each time Kit and Ket had met, they were separated by some invisible occult curse and yet, by the grace of the all-powerful Supreme Being, their love endured and remained undiminished. The family reunion of Ket, Sook and Soor with Kit evoked a rare deluge of love and happiness on the soils of Hunthad. The ripples of this deluge reached every Hunthadian heart and quenched their souls.

Soor accompanied her father, Kit, to the mouth of the *well of death*. Her very advent changed the gravity of the place. The filth in the air gave way to the fragrance of her pure being. Dry grey tufts of grassy alien plants around the well became green. Flowers blossomed on the shrubs in all their hues and shades calling the six-winged *rainbow flies* with the promise of renewed nectar.

One by one, the battered spirits of the condemned *sobers* came out of the well. Their agonies, harboured over millennia, were instantaneously soothed at the very sight of the endearing innocent smile on Soor's face and by the soul quenching sound of her, sweeter than the cuckoo, voice. With the bondage to their agonies cut asunder, the ancient spirits moved upwards into the sky to be released in the ever peaceful realm of the Supreme.

Before leaving Hunthad, Kit inaugurated a statue of Jik, the martyr, who, like many other *sobers*, had given up his life to usher in the realisation of the more *universal and inclusive* aspects and the *higher ideals* of the *yellow colour.*

23

THE RETURN

So, Kit had opened the door to unity between Inthad and Isthad; enhanced the possibilities of harmony among Hunthad and the other *colour countries* dispelling the veil of one stereotyped illusion after another from the collective consciousness of the Hoo race. However, his dream of bringing about the *psychic harmony among the Hoo race* was far from being materialised. The great work, which Kit had set out to accomplish, had just begun and was anything but over. There were yet more hurdles in the way to awakening among the race the awareness about their global existence. *Old habits die hard and ancient habits, passed on through the generations over millennia, die extremely hard.*

Kit would wisely say, "Each Hoo mistakes its partial *colour perception* to be the perception of the *Whole*. This is the root cause of all *Colour Differences*."

I eagerly anticipated witnessing Kit's heroic endeavors to conquer the remaining hurdles to his dream. But, destiny had other things in store for me. It suddenly happened one day.

That day, I had accompanied Kit and his family on a picnic party to our favourite spot by the dried up Forbidden River at the foot of the Forbidden Mountain.

The wonder kids, Sook and Soor, were merry at a Hoo game. The lovebirds, Kit and Ket, were engrossed with each other. I decided to take a stroll along the bank of the Forbidden River in the panoramic violet scenario under the bright afternoon sky.

Out of nowhere, a thunderous bolt struck a few feet ahead of me defying the clear sky and breaking the serene quiet of the place. A circular screen of rippling white light appeared before me. As incredible as the screen was, it looked incredibly beautiful. Before I knew it, I had curiously touched the screen with my left hand. My hand easily went into the screen. Then I felt that the screen was pulling me by my hand. I did not know what was there in the screen. Horrified and struggling to free myself off the screen, I looked backwards and cried out, "Ki …t."

All four of the family had surely noticed the extraordinary phenomenon. They had hurried towards me. I saw them standing a few feet behind me, the kids flanked by their parents. They appeared calm. Kit serenely said, "Don't be afraid, Doctor. It is time for you to return to your planet, Earth. Tell your people about your experiences on Hoola. We will ever cherish your fond memories. Adieu, my friend."

All four smiled and waved at me. I smiled back and bade them farewell. The increasing pull of the screen became overwhelming. I gave in and was instantaneously sucked up into the screen.

* * *

The next thing I remember is that, I found myself lying on the bank of a gushing and gurgling river with plenty of greenery around. Interestingly, I had the same clothes on, which I had been wearing on the day of my car accident. My attire looked dirty. I gently got up and looked around to guess my location. All I could see was virgin green forest on both sides of the river. So, I decided to walk down the river to find civilisation. Before long, I was noticed and picked up by a group of adventure seeking river rafters. They brought me back to our asylum.

My colleagues and friends were happy to see me alive. But they opined that, along with my car, I had accidentally fallen into the river that flows through the ravine. The rarely ever seen reclusive aboriginal tribes, who are supposed to live in the dense vegetation and inaccessible recesses of the reserve forests in and around the ravine, must have taken care of me for seven months while I was unconscious. Then, when I was a little better, they left me on the bank of the river.

My friends took my visit to Hoola for an unconscious dream. Whatever they may think, it is amazing for me that Earth has grown only seven months older while I spent several years on Hoola. My physicist friend had once told me that, under certain conditions, it is possible to come back even in the past after a space travel.

24 AFTER WORDS

As a psychologist, I am aware that the scope of the human mind, in spite of having endless potentials, is, in reality, finite and not unlimited. There is a general tendency in most of us to try to accommodate everything within that *finiteness*. The ocean of knowledge, however, is infinite. The problem arises when the human mind comes across something which is higher, greater and beyond its scope. First, the mind tries to correlate that *beyond-ness* with something which it already knows. But this is impossible because the only way to comprehend and grasp the *beyond-ness* is to grow up to the higher and greater *beyond-ness*. This requires perseverance and patience, the two qualities which are often wanting. So the impatient mind seeks a quick shortcut. Most of us exhibit a general tendency to try to reduce the *beyond-ness* and thus degenerate it into something smaller which we can then associate and accommodate in our minds.

My people here, in order to explain my disappearance for long seven months, are more willing to conjecture upon the theory of these aboriginal tribes, whom they have never seen, than believe me and my first hand, even if apparently fantastic, experiences on the planet, Hoola. Their already rationally stereotyped human minds seek evidence which I do not have. There is no way I can make them believe me. The more I try, the more I will be taken for a lunatic. So I have decided to remain quiet about my visit to Hoola. I strongly believe that, the experiences, which I gathered on Hoola could provide useful food for thought and be immensely beneficial to us, the Earthlings, but alas, to no avail. I do not want to become an inmate myself. I do not want to lose my freedom. But, how can I disbelieve my own experiences just because these people would like me to do so? That would be like denying my own existence. So, I have secretly written this book for your delight and discernibility.

Now I realise how Kit must have felt over two long decades, while he was an inmate in our asylum, each time he repeated and reiterated the truth that only he knew the best and we thought that he was crazy. I feel relieved though that, at least in my consciousness there is a great chance that not only Kit and his incredible family but the entire Hoo-manity, indeed lives happily ever after on their spectacular multi-coloured planet Hoola, in their own space and time.